Silvermist

and the

Ladybird Curse

&

A Masterpiece

for Bess

PaRragon
Bath · New York · Singapore · Hong Kong · Cologne · Delhi · Melbourne

All About Fairies

IF YOU HEAD towards the second star on your right and fly straight on till morning, you'll come to Never Land, a magical island where mermaids play and children never grow up.

When you arrive, you might hear something like the tinkling of little bells. Follow that sound and you'll find Pixie Hollow, the secret heart of Never Land.

A great old maple tree grows in Pixie Hollow, and in it live hundreds of fairies and sparrow men. Some of them can do water magic, others can fly like the wind, and still others can speak to animals. You see, Pixie Hollow is the Never fairies' kingdom, and each fairy who lives there has a special, extraordinary talent.

Not far from the Home Tree, nestled in the branches of a hawthorn, is Mother Dove, the most magical creature of all. She sits on her egg, watching over the fairies, who in turn watch over her. For as long as Mother Dove's egg stays well and whole, no one in Never Land will ever grow old.

Once, Mother Dove's egg *was* broken. But we are not telling the story of the egg here. Now it is time for Silvermist's and Bess's tales. . . .

Silvermist
and the
Ladybird
Curse

WRITTEN BY
GAIL HERMAN

ILLUSTRATED BY
ADRIENNE BROWN, CHARLES PICKENS
& DENISE SHIMABUKURO

First published by Parragon in 2009
Parragon
Queen Street House
4 Queen Street
Bath BA1 1HE, UK

ISBN 978-1-4075-2221-0

Printed in China

SUNLIGHT SPARKLED ON the cool, clear waters of Havendish Stream. Silvermist waded in. She took the oak-leaf cover off her tiny birchbark canoe.

She lifted her face and sniffed the air. "Mmmm-mmmm."

Silvermist was a water-talent fairy. She loved everything about water: the sight, the sounds, and the feel of it. And she especially loved the damp, sharp smell of it.

But this day, the smells of freshly baked muffins and cakes were mixed in with the smell of the stream. The fairies and sparrow men of Pixie Hollow were getting ready for a picnic – a special picnic on an island not far from the shore. Water fairies filled birchbark canoes with food, drinks, and supplies.

Grass-weaving talents carried picnic blankets. Harvest talents brought fresh berries. Baking talents flew over to the boats with picnic treats.

Silvermist smiled as she stepped back to the shore. "It all smells delicious!" she told Dulcie, a baking talent. "This picnic will be the best ever."

Dulcie nodded. She held out a basket for Silvermist to take. "Here are some muffins and berry juice."

"I'll help!" said Silvermist's friend Fira, a light-talent fairy, as she reached for the basket to put into the canoe.

Silvermist smiled at Fira. Some fairies thought it odd that they were friends. The two were so different. Fira was quick tempered and fiery, while Silvermist was calm and quiet.

They were opposites, but they were

drawn to each other.

Rani, another water talent, pushed off in her canoe. She began to paddle towards the island.

One by one, the rest of the water fairies followed. The Fairy Ferry was under way. Other talents hovered above the canoes. They trailed the boats towards the island.

"Come on, Silvermist!" Fira said. "You're going to be late!"

"I know. But I promised Iris I would take something for her," Silvermist replied. "I'll just wait a bit longer."

Iris, a garden-talent fairy, wanted to bring flowers to the picnic. None of the other fairies thought that was necessary. After all, there would be all sorts of flowers growing on the island. But Iris had insisted.

"Okay, Silvermist. But hurry," Fira said. "Right now is the perfect time for a picnic. It's almost high noon. The sun will be right over our heads."

Silvermist watched Fira join the others. Then she settled back and took in the scene. It all looked so lovely. The canoes drifted in rows while the fairies flew gracefully above. Silvermist didn't want to miss any of the picnic. *But if I'm going to be late anyway,* she thought, *I may as well relax.*

"Silvermist! Silvermist!" Iris rushed up with an armful of messy-looking wildflowers. As usual, her long narrow nose was red at the tip. "Here I am!"

She stood the flowers at the back of the canoe. "Phew! That took a while. But I knew you wouldn't leave before I got here!"

Silvermist glanced over at the flowers. "What are they?"

"They are very rare chrysanthepoppies. I searched every field in Pixie

Hollow just to find them."

"Chrysanthe-poppies?" Silvermist had never heard of them.

"Here, I'll show you!" Iris flipped open her huge book about flowers.

Iris was the only garden fairy who didn't have her own garden. Instead, she put all her energy into writing her plant book. She claimed to be an expert on every plant, flower, and seed in Never Land.

Silvermist examined the flowers. Honestly, they looked more like weeds than anything else. But taking these flowers to the picnic meant a lot to Iris. So Silvermist was happy to help her.

"I'm going now!" Iris said as she flew away. "Don't bump the canoe too much, Silvermist. The flowers are very delicate!"

Silvermist paddled away from the shore. Most of the other fairies were already on the island. But the day was so beautiful, Silvermist decided to take her time and enjoy the trip.

"Moving a bit slowly today, sweetheart?" asked Vidia, a fast-flying fairy, as she landed lightly on the end of Silvermist's canoe.

Vidia gave Silvermist her usual smirk. It showed a mix of scorn and boredom. Vidia always acted as if she had someplace better to be and somebody better to be with.

"Are you going to the picnic?" Silvermist asked, though she already knew the answer. Vidia didn't bother much with fairy gatherings.

"Me?" Vidia laughed. "Goodness, no. I just happened to be flying by, and I saw all these fairies happily picnicking on the island. You, however, sweetie, seem to have . . . ahem . . . missed the boat. I thought water fairies were skilled at paddling. Are you feeling all right?" Vidia's voice was full of fake concern.

"I'm fine, Vidia," Silvermist said. She was nearing the island. Fira waved to her from the shore.

"Fine?" Vidia repeated. "There's nothing fine about going at a snail's pace. I've never seen a water fairy paddle so slowly."

Silvermist just shrugged. She continued to move at the same speed.

Vidia frowned. Usually she could get a rise out of fairies. But her words had no effect on Silvermist. "Whatever could be —"

"How are my flowers doing?" Iris shouted to Silvermist from the water's edge.

"Flowers? Is that what those weeds are?" Vidia leaned over to peer at the untidy bundle.

The canoe tipped.

"Oh!" Vidia cried. Her feet slipped out from under her, and she fell backwards. Her wings dipped into the stream. They soaked up water like a sea sponge. Try as she might, Vidia couldn't find her balance again.

Vidia fell into the water with a loud splash.

"Help! Help!" Iris shouted. "My picnic flowers are ruined. And Vidia's drowning!"

2

Vidia flailed in the stream. The water continued to seep into her wings, dragging her down.

"Hang on, Vidia! I'll get you!" Silvermist cried. She dropped to her knees and reached out.

Vidia waved her arms in alarm. "Calm down!" Silvermist shouted. "I can't get hold of you!"

"Help! Help!" Iris shrieked loudly from the shore.

A crowd of fairies flew over. Quickly, they pulled Vidia out of the water.

"Look at this!" Rani said. She waded into the stream. "It's not deep at all! The water doesn't even reach up to my waist!"

Sitting on the sandy beach, Vidia glared at Rani. Her glow turned bright red.

"That's a good joke on you, Vidia,"

Prilla said with a giggle. "You could have just stood up!"

Silvermist's canoe bumped against the shore. She climbed out.

"Shush, everyone!" Silvermist hurried over to Vidia. "Are you all right?" she asked.

Silvermist's heartfelt concern seemed to annoy Vidia even more than the teasing did.

"I'm f-f-fine," Vidia said. Her teeth chattered. She was shivering from the cool water. "I was balancing p-p-perfectly well. But then you had to squirm around and rock the boat."

"How can you blame Silvermist?" Tink asked.

Vidia raised her eyebrows. "Oh, please! I d-d-didn't arrive yesterday. You don't think I'd just fall in, d-d-do you?"

"Accidents happen," Silvermist said.

"Not to me," Vidia snapped. She glared

at the surrounding fairies. "Why don't you go back to your l-l-little picnic!"

Fira shrugged and wandered away with the other fairies. Only Silvermist remained. "Do you need a blanket?" she asked. "Or something to eat?"

Vidia shook her dripping wings. Then she stood and drew herself up to her full five inches.

"If I could, Silvermist, sweetheart, I'd f-f-fly away right now. But since I'm stuck at this s-s-s-silly picnic until my wings dry, I'll manage fine."

Vidia tossed her long, wet ponytail and turned away. Silvermist sat with Fira and Tinker Bell. She ate berries and tiny watercress sandwiches. Every now and then, she glanced over at Vidia.

She felt terrible about what had

happened. No fairy liked to have water-logged wings. And she knew that Vidia hated to be made fun of. Still, Silvermist found herself enjoying the picnic.

As soon as she finished eating, cleanup talents whisked away her plate. Fira stood up and said, "We have hours before sunset. What should we do?"

Beck, an animal-talent fairy, jumped to her feet. "I know! Let's play spots and dots!" she said.

Silvermist smiled. She hadn't played that game in a while.

Beck cupped her hands around her mouth like a megaphone. Then she made a loud clicking noise with her tongue.

A moment later, dozens of ladybirds flew to her side. She whispered to the bugs. She was making sure they wanted to play.

"Now, does everyone remember the

rules?" she asked the fairies. "We give the ladybirds ten seconds to hide. You have to find as many ladybirds as you can and count the dots on their backs. Whoever scores highest wins!"

She handed out lily pads and berry-ink pens to record the spots and dots. "Ready?"

"Ready!" shouted everyone but Vidia.

"Count!"

Silvermist began counting slowly with the others. "One Pixie Hollow. Two Pixie Hollow. Three . . ." As they counted, the ladybirds flew off to hide.

As soon as the fairies and sparrow men reached ten, they darted away. They flew here and there, trying to find as many lady-birds as they could.

Silvermist trailed the others. She wasn't in a hurry. She checked every hiding place . . . every nook . . . every cranny. She looked under every leaf and behind every rock.

She found one ladybird between the roots of a hickory tree, and another in the dense branches of a mulberry bush. A third was hiding in a bird's nest.

Silvermist sat under a shady leaf to add up her points. *Wait a minute!* she thought. She saw a silhouette through the leaf. It was shaped like a ladybird!

This could be it – the one that would give her more points than any other fairy! She stepped away from the leaf for a better look.

It *was* a ladybird. But it was the strangest ladybird Silvermist had ever seen. It was milky white, from tip to tip.

Its spots were difficult to see. They were white, too, just a shade darker than the rest of the ladybird – and there must have been a dozen of them!

She'd found a ladybird with the most dots she'd ever counted! Surely, she'd win the game.

Silvermist looked down to tally her score. As she did, the white ladybird hopped onto her head.

"Hey!" she called out to the other fairies. "Do I get extra points if a ladybird finds *me*?"

Beck and Fawn hurried over. "A white ladybird!" Beck peered up at the insect. "I've never seen one before!"

"It's very rare," Fawn agreed.

By now, other fairies had gathered around Silvermist. The ladybird sat perfectly still atop the water-talent fairy's head.

"You know," a garden fairy named Rosetta mused, "there's an old superstition about white ladybirds. They're supposed to bring—"

"Bad luck!" Iris said, screeching to a stop in front of Silvermist.

A few fairies chuckled uncertainly. No one took Iris very seriously. But fairies were superstitious creatures. They believed in wishes, charms, and luck – both good and bad.

"The white ladybird!" Iris's voice rose higher and higher. "It's cursed!"

3

A HUSH FELL over the picnic site. All around Silvermist, fairies stopped playing. They stopped talking. They even stopped moving.

Silvermist shook her head. She hoped the ladybird would fly away. But it didn't. It just settled more comfortably in place.

"Oh, this is bad," Iris moaned. "A cursed white ladybird. Make it go away!"

A murmur went through the crowd. Some fairies gasped.

"Stop that, Iris!" Fira spoke sharply. "You're scaring everyone."

"She's not *scaring* me," Silvermist said. "But going around with a ladybird on my head will be a bother."

"Here, let us help." Beck flew closer, with Fawn by her side. Gently, they lifted the bug and carried it to a tree.

The ladybird paused for a moment. Then it flew up and disappeared among the leaves.

"Well." Silvermist looked around at the other fairies. "That was a little strange."

Iris backed away from her. She had a wild look in her eye. "It's not just strange, Silvermist. It's bad, as in bad luck. A white ladybird is bad luck. And to have one land on your head? That's the worst possible luck."

Slowly, the fairies turned to one another. Their voices were hushed but urgent. "Silvermist has been touched by a white ladybird!" "It's bad luck!" "She's cursed!"

Silvermist couldn't believe it. Everyone was scared of a harmless ladybird? And why? Because of a foolish myth?

Silvermist shrugged. "I don't really believe in those old fairy superstitions."

She smiled at Fira and her other friends. She was expecting to see nods of agreement. She thought they'd say, "Yes, we know exactly what you mean." Instead, everyone was silent. The island was quiet, too. No birds cooed. No bees buzzed.

Everyone stared at Silvermist. They had frightened looks on their faces. Finally, Fira spoke. "I don't know, Silvermist . . ."

Iris's nose turned even redder than usual. "What's not to know?" she shouted. "Everyone saw it! Right on Silvermist's head!"

"Let's stay calm," Rani said. She sounded nervous, though. "Let's not think the worst."

"I'm not thinking any such thing. And I

am calm, Silvermist said in a level voice. "There's no such thing as bad luck."

Humidia wiped away a tear. "Are you sure?" she asked weepily.

"Yes, I'm sure. The curse means nothing. It's an old fairy tale . . . like 'step on a crack, break a sparrow man's back.' Right, Terence?"

"Right!" the dust-talent sparrow man said, a little too quickly. He thumped himself on the back. "Not one broken bone!"

"So!" Silvermist grinned at her friends. "I'm not going to pay attention to this crazy superstition. And neither should anyone else."

"The curse is real!" Iris insisted. "Why, back when I had my own garden . . ."

Everyone sighed. Iris was always going on about the good old days, when she had the most amazing garden in all of Pixie Hollow. They were tired of hearing it. They turned away.

"Maybe we should go back to the Home Tree," Terence suggested. "You could get some rest, Silvermist."

"Yes," Rani agreed. "You must be feeling . . . strange."

Everyone else is acting *strange,* Silvermist thought. She felt just as she always did. And she'd been having such fun. She didn't want it to end.

"Really, I'm fine," she told the others.

Fira stepped forward. "Do you know what I think?"

Silvermist caught her breath. Fira looked serious. Did she believe in the curse, too?

"I think we should play fairy tag," Fira finished.

Silvermist smiled. She knew she could count on her friend.

"So you want to play?" Tink asked.

"Of course!" Silvermist said.

"Then . . ." Fira tapped Silvermist on the head. "Choose you!"

"Water talents are chosen!" Rani declared.

For a moment, no one moved. Not even Silvermist. Then she fluttered a wing.

Fairies scattered in all directions.

The water talents dashed here and there, trying to chase fairies from different talents.

Silvermist hovered above the beach. *Let's see*, she thought. *Which fairy should I tag?*

She spied Beck just a short distance away. Beck was flying around a beehive. She wasn't looking behind her.

"This should be easy!" Silvermist said to herself. All thoughts of the white lady-bird and the curse were already far from her mind.

She neared the beehive just as Beck swung around.

Beck laughed. She had nowhere to go. Tree branches blocked her every move. Quickly, she flew into a knothole.

"You can't escape that way, Beck!" Silvermist called playfully. She flew after her friend.

"Yoo-hoo, Silvermist!" Fawn called. "What about me?"

"Fawn?" Silvermist turned her head. And in that split second, she missed the knothole and crashed right into the tree trunk.

"Ouch!" She fluttered to the ground.

"Hurry! Hurry!" Fawn cried. "We need

healing talents. Now!"

Silvermist rubbed her forehead. Already, a pea-sized bump was forming on it.

"Do you need a leaf compress? An icy-water pack?" asked Clara, the first healing talent to arrive.

Silvermist tried to shake her head. "Ouch!" she said again. "Well, maybe the pack," she admitted. Clara handed her a pink petal-pouch full of water. Silvermist held it in her hand for a moment, helping the pack freeze. Then Clara placed the icy pack on the bump.

"Are you all right?" Fira asked, landing beside Silvermist. "What happened to you?"

"I'm fine, Fira. I just missed a knothole and hit the tree instead."

Fira lifted the pack to check the bump.

"That doesn't look fine to me." She lowered her voice. "Do you . . . do you think it could be the curse?"

"No, Fira. I don't." Silvermist spoke in an even tone. "It was just an accident. A regular, everyday sort of accident. Like I told Vidia, accidents happen. Any fairy could have done it."

"Any fairy?" Vidia flew over. Her wings were finally dry. She circled above everyone and shot a triumphant look at Silvermist. Her glow had lost its embarrassed pink tinge. She tossed her head, proud as ever.

"Any fairy would fly right into a big old tree? I don't think so." Vidia clucked with false concern. "No, sweetie, a fairy needs to be pretty unlucky to do that."

4

Unlucky? Silvermist didn't feel unlucky, despite what Vidia said. Any fairy could have a little flying accident. Any fairy could turn her head for just an instant and fly into something, even a tree.

"It's nothing to worry about," she told herself. "There is no curse."

Still, she knew that the other fairies were whispering. They were saying she'd had bad luck. They were saying she was cursed.

But I don't believe it, Silvermist thought. *Not now. Not ever.*

The picnic wasn't over yet, but Silvermist didn't feel like returning to it. Instead, she flew to the seashore to watch the ocean waves. She wanted to be alone. She didn't want to hear the fairy gossip.

Hours passed. When the tide went out, it left small pools of water scattered around the shore. Silvermist flew from tidal pool to tidal pool, looking for hermit crabs and tiny fish.

Then something caught her eye. A sparkling object was lying on the beach. Was it a shiny rock? A piece of sea glass? She flitted closer. It was a seashell! The tiniest, most perfect shell she'd ever seen.

Silvermist picked it up. Its inside was orange with wavy lines that spread out like rays of sunshine. Silvermist knew that it was special. Just holding it made her feel better.

Let the fairies and sparrow men talk of curses and bad luck. She didn't care.

She slipped the shell into a fold of her dress and flew back toward the Home Tree.

When she got there, Silvermist flew on to the tearoom. It was empty. Next door, in the kitchen, baking and cooking talents were hard at work, preparing the evening meal.

Silvermist was too early for dinner. But maybe she could help in the kitchen. She would see if the cooking fairies needed help boiling water.

She ducked through the swinging door. Fairies flitted around the room, mixing, beating, sprinkling, and stirring. Two sparrow men stood by the sink, rinsing dirt off a big carrot.

"Dulcie!" Silvermist called. "Is there anything I can do?"

Dulcie was kneading dough at the big table in the centre of the room. "Well, I don't know," she said, a little uneasily. "Are you feeling okay? Is your bump all healed?"

"All better," Silvermist declared.

"That's good. But there's really nothing

for you to do here, Silvermist." Dulcie nodded at the stove. Three pots of water were already boiling merrily. "You don't even have to come inside. Really."

She's nervous about my being here, Silvermist realized. *She's afraid I'll bring bad luck or have another accident. I have to show her that nothing has changed. I'm the same water fairy I've always been.*

"What about those pitchers?" she asked. Rows of water pitchers lined a long table across the room from the sink. "I could fill them for you."

"I don't think—" Dulcie began.

But Silvermist was already at the water pump. She caught the water as it flowed. Then, with a gentle underhand toss, she sent it streaming over Dulcie's head and into the first pitcher.

Not one drop spilled.

"See?" Silvermist grinned triumphantly. "I can do this quickly, while the carrot is being washed."

On the other side of the swinging doors, fairies were heading into the tearoom for dinner. "Well, it *would* help move things along," Dulcie admitted.

At that moment, Vidia swept into the kitchen. "I was just flying past. You know, normally I like to dine alone. But I saw you here, Silvermist, and I had to drop in and see how you were."

"Oh?" Silvermist concentrated on the next pitcher of water.

"Yes." Vidia made herself comfortable in a chair next to Dulcie. "You were at the picnic, weren't you, Dulcie, dear? So you know about poor Silvermist and the ladybird?"

Dulcie nodded.

"Well, I just wanted to make sure she hadn't had any other—" Vidia paused to make sure she had Silvermist's full attention – "unfortunate accidents."

"Nope." Silvermist shot another expert stream into the next pitcher. "Not one."

Vidia gave her a tight-lipped smile. "Good," she said. She sounded as if she meant the opposite. "Although, not much time has passed, really. Anything could happen. You know, you can't ignore the magic behind these old tales. Just the other day, I heard about a butterfly herder. He forgot to cross his wings before passing the skeleton tree . . ."

Dulcie had stopped working. She turned to Vidia, taking in every word. The other fairies and sparrow men leaned closer, straining to hear.

". . . and the next thing he knew, his

entire herd of butterflies had flown off. He never found them!" said Vidia.

Silvermist tried not to listen. She kept quietly filling pitchers.

"And there was that sparrow man who broke some sea glass," Vidia went on. "He had seven hundred years of bad luck. At least that's what everyone thinks. But no one ever saw him after year five thirty-nine."

She stole a glance at Silvermist.

"And there was a garden-talent fairy who opened a petal umbrella inside the Home Tree. Well, right after that, she planted a carrot seed – or so she thought. Turned out she'd planted the seed of a snareweed plant. When the thing sprouted, it nearly ate her!"

Silvermist's hands were steady as she worked. She stayed calm, even as Vidia's stories grew more and more outrageous. But really, she couldn't wait to finish. All that talk about bad luck and curses! She wanted it to end.

"I'm done," Silvermist said. She crossed the kitchen to check the water level in the pitchers. "Looks okay to me," she announced. "What do you think, Dulcie?"

"Perfect!" Dulcie declared.

"See? Not one accident," Silvermist couldn't resist saying to Vidia. "I guess I'll go into the tearoom now."

Silvermist turned. Her wing brushed against a pitcher. The pitcher tipped and fell against another pitcher. Then that pitcher tipped, knocking over a third that fell against a fourth that tumbled into a fifth.

Silvermist tried to catch them, but she wasn't quick enough. Pitcher after pitcher toppled. And fast-flying Vidia didn't move a muscle to help. She just sat there, smiling.

Silvermist gazed at the kitchen. Water had spilled everywhere. It had splashed onto the honey buns and into the walnut soup. It poured over plates and cups and across the floor. Fairies rushed around the room with moss mops and towels.

"Hmmm," Vidia said. "Looks like dinner might be late tonight. What do you think, Silvermist?"

5

THE TEAROOM WAS filled with fairies and sparrow men. Each one stared at the swinging doors to the kitchen. They were all waiting for dinner.

Dulcie flew through the kitchen doors. "The meal will be served late," she announced.

At the water-talent table, Silvermist ducked her head. She knew that it was her fault dinner was late.

But Dulcie and the others will work their kitchen magic, she thought. *Everyone will be eating delicious food in no time.* There was no reason to be upset.

Minutes later, the serving talents brought out steaming bowls of acorn soup and sunflower stew. It *was* delicious.

Silvermist had been right. The accident wasn't anything to worry about. Not really.

Just then, Vidia flew to the fast-flying talent table. She was so rarely in the tearoom that she had nowhere to sit. "No, no, don't get up," she said, even though no one was offering a chair. "I'm not staying, darlings. I just wanted to make sure those gossipy serving talents weren't spreading any rumours."

The serving talents stopped their work to look at Vidia. Not one of them had been talking. They'd been moving so quickly to serve dinner, they hadn't had time to say a word.

Now all eyes were on Vidia.

Vidia cast a look at Silvermist, making sure everyone noticed. "I wouldn't want any fairy to be the subject of idle gossip," she went on. "But . . ." She stretched out the word meaningfully.

Iris leaped to her feet. "Something happened to Silvermist! I knew it! What, Vidia? Was it another accident?"

Fairies and sparrow men swivelled in their seats to stare at Silvermist.

"I'll answer that." Silvermist's voice was steady. "I spilled some water, Iris. It was just a little spill."

"Is that what you'd call it, darling?" Vidia asked.

A voice rang out from the kitchen. "Cleanup talents! We need help in the pantry! The flour is soaked! The spices are drenched! The fruit is soggy! It's a mess!"

Silvermist looked calmly back at Vidia. She felt bad about causing the mess. But really, the whole idea of the curse was so silly. Why not make a joke of it?

"Maybe I *would* call it a little spill," she

answered Vidia with a laugh. "And maybe I'd call Torth Mountain an anthill."

Across the room, Fira chuckled. "And maybe the sun is just a firefly torch," she added.

"And the Home Tree is a little sapling," said Rosetta.

Soon, everyone was joining in the game. It seemed they'd all forgotten about the accident.

Silvermist kept thinking about it, though. An image flashed through her mind: pitcher after pitcher falling over.

Yes, she'd managed to laugh off the spill. But what about her flying accident? Was there something to what Vidia had said? Did the old fairy tales have a powerful magic?

She glanced at Vidia, who was standing by the fast-flying table. She looked like she knew what Silvermist was thinking. Vidia gave her a slow, cruel smile. And with a flick of her ponytail, she flew out of the tearoom.

Dessert berries were on the tables now. Dinner would be over soon. Silvermist reached for the sugar bowl.

"Oops!" She knocked over the pepper shaker. The top popped off. Pepper scattered across the table. Silvermist hoped no one had noticed. But no such luck.

"Oh!" Iris moaned. "Spilled pepper? That's bad luck, too!"

"Quick!" Fira said. "Toss some over your left shoulder!"

Silvermist scooped up a handful of pepper. Without thinking, she threw it over her shoulder . . . right into the face of a serving talent who was carrying a platter of almond pudding.

"Watch out!" Rosetta cried. But it was

too late.

The serving talent sneezed. The platter flipped. Pudding flew everywhere.

Another disaster, Silvermist thought with a groan.

It seemed that all the fairies and sparrow men had lost their appetites. One by one, they filed quietly out of the tea-room.

Fira stopped to give Silvermist a quick hug.

"I'll just sit here a little longer," Silvermist told her. Fira nodded and went on her way.

Alone and confused, Silvermist sighed. The tree and water accidents weren't as easy to explain away any- more. Not after the pepper mishap.

Maybe I truly am unlucky, she thought. *Maybe the curse is real.*

6

Silvermist felt better after a good night's sleep. In the morning light, the talk of bad luck seemed silly.

She flung open her window to let in the fresh air.

Chirp, ch-ch-chirp! A cricket hopped onto a branch outside her window. He rubbed his back legs together, chirping.

The music was so sweet, so soothing. Silvermist smiled. *The cricket is singing just for me*, she thought.

Silvermist sat down next to the window. She listened to the cricket for a long time.

If she were really unlucky, would this be happening? Would a cricket give her a private concert?

With one final chirp, the cricket

hopped away.

Humming his song under her breath, Silvermist flew out to the courtyard. It seemed every fairy and sparrow man in Pixie Hollow was returning from somewhere.

"Wasn't that amazing?" asked Fawn, rushing over to Silvermist. "If I tried, I couldn't organize a concert like that."

Does Fawn mean the cricket by my window? Silvermist wondered. *But how would she know about that?*

"All those songbirds," Fawn went on. "There must have been thirty of them! All singing so sweetly. It was like nothing I've ever heard. Why they landed in the fairy circle to sing, I'll never know."

Beck joined them. "I don't think we'll

see something like that again. Not for years and years – if ever!"

Slowly, Silvermist began to understand. There had been a songbird concert. An unexpected, wonderful performance, the likes of which no one had heard before. And she'd missed it.

Suddenly, Silvermist's private concert didn't seem so special. She didn't feel very lucky at all.

"Oh, Silvermist!" Fira rushed over. "You weren't there!"

"I know." If only she had woken up sooner, she might have seen the concert. Wouldn't anything go right for her?

Just then, she remembered something that *had* gone right. "Wait a minute!" she said to Fira. "I have something to show you!"

Her special seashell. The one she'd

found on the beach. Just remembering it made Silvermist feel better. She reached into the fold of her dress.

It was empty. "Oh!" she gasped. "Where is it?" She felt around every inch of the fabric.

One of her fingers poked out through the bottom.

Her dress had a hole. The seashell had fallen out, Silvermist realized. She could search and search, but what good would it do? She'd never find it.

She wasn't the kind of fairy who found lost things anymore. She was the kind of fairy who flew into trees. And tipped over water pitchers. And ruined desserts. And missed songbirds.

Silvermist *was* unlucky. She was cursed. There was no doubt about it.

Word spread quickly through the Home

Tree. Silvermist had missed the best concert in Pixie Hollow history – just because she had been late!

"I told you! I told you! She's cursed!" Iris said, fluttering from fairy to fairy.

With Iris moaning and crying, everyone looked worried. It was hard for Silvermist to stay calm. Her glow flared bright orange with embarrassment.

"Ahem!" Rani cleared her throat. "I have an announcement to make," she said, thinking quickly. Fairies shifted their attention. Silvermist's glow faded. She smiled at Rani gratefully.

"There will be a waterball tournament in two days," Rani said. "All are welcome to watch. And all water talents are invited to show their skills."

A waterball tournament! Silvermist loved contests. She enjoyed matching throws with her friends and aiming waterballs at targets. But she couldn't do it now. With her luck, the tournament would be a disaster.

"I'll be there!" Humidia declared.

"So will I!" another water talent called out.

"I'm sure Silvermist won't be taking part," Vidia said, "due to a severe case of bad luck."

What? Silvermist turned to frown at her. Vidia couldn't speak for her! True, she'd been thinking the very same thing. But for Vidia to say what she should do . . . well, that was unacceptable!

"Vidia is mistaken," Silvermist said. "I will be there." She smiled at Rani.

The water talents cheered. Silvermist knew she had done the right thing.

There was only one problem. Like Vidia had said, anything could happen.

7

"Oh, why did I say I'd do it?" Silvermist asked Fira. She felt funny. Nervous and uneasy. And to be honest, she even felt a little panicky. For Silvermist, this was strange indeed.

"Why did I ever say I'd be in the tournament?" Silvermist moaned. "I just know something's going to go terribly wrong."

Silvermist and Fira were leaving the courtyard. "We'll think of something," Fira said as they flew through the halls of the Home Tree.

"Hey! Wait!" The light-talent fairy skidded to a stop in front of the Home Tree library. "Let's go in here.

The library has lots of books on superstitions. It might give us an idea."

Well, Silvermist thought, *it's better than*

doing nothing.

"Okay," she agreed.

Inside, Fira led Silvermist to a far corner. A small sign read LUCK: GOOD AND BAD. The entire section – bookcase after bookcase – held books about superstition.

"I never knew this was here," said Silvermist .

"Of course not," Fira replied. "You never thought to look."

Fira brought Silvermist to a shelf marked Bugs and Insects. Silvermist flipped open one book. It had two chapters on the rare white ladybird. The next book had three chapters. And another was simply titled Beware the White Ladybird.

Silvermist began to read.

"'Good-luck charms and bad-luck curses are all around us. And perhaps the most powerful of all, is the curse cast by the white ladybird.'"

Silvermist gasped. Most powerful? A lump formed in her throat. "Oh, Fira. It's the worst curse of all. What can I do? It's hopeless!"

Fira leaped up to comfort her. "It doesn't have to be hopeless! Look at all these other books."

Fira pulled another book off the shelf. The title was *Never Bad Luck/ Always Good Luck.*

"You mean, I might be able to undo the curse with a good-luck charm?" Silvermist asked.

Fira grinned at her friend. "Let's find out!"

Silvermist and Fira read through the night. By early the next morning, they had put together a list called Things to Do to Bring Good Luck.

Silvermist sighed. "Do you think I can really drive away the curse?"

"Of course! We just have to find the right charm," Fira said.

Silvermist read the first good-luck charm on the list. "'Circle the Home Tree anti-clockwise seven times under a blue moon.' When is the next blue moon?" she asked.

"Next year," Fira told her.

Silvermist crossed that item off the list. She'd have to try another one. "Okay, number two: 'Find a five-leaf clover.'"

Silvermist pictured all the fields and meadows in Pixie Hollow. Surely, there must be a five-leaf clover hidden with in them. But how long would it take to check all those places? The tournament was the next day. It seemed too risky.

She read the next item on the list. "'Spot a triple rainbow.'"

It was a bright, sunny day. There was

little chance of seeing any rainbow, let alone a triple one.

Finally, she read, "'Find a pin and pick it up.'"

That sounds simple," Fira said. "Sewing-talents are always using pins."

"Right," Silvermist agreed. "Let's find a sewing fairy, then."

"And ask her for a pin?"

Silvermist thought for a moment, then shook her head. "That wouldn't exactly be finding one, would it?"

"What if we follow her," Fira suggested, "and if she drops one, you can pick it up!"

Silvermist grinned. "And get good luck!"

The two friends hurried from the library. They circled the entrance hall and the tearoom. But it was early. Hardly anyone was about. They didn't see a single sewing talent.

They flew up to the floor where most of the sewing talents had their rooms.

Just then, Hem fluttered into the hallway. Silvermist nudged Fira and pointed. The pockets on Hem's sewing apron were stuffed with needles and pins.

"Time to check those spiderwebs," Hem was muttering. "See if they're clean and ready for the queen's gown."

"She's going to the laundry room," Fira hissed to Silvermist.

Hem flew down through the Home Tree, heading towards the lowest floor. Silvermist and Fira followed quietly.

On the sixth floor, Hem glanced over her left shoulder. In a flash, Silvermist and Fira ducked into a supply cupboard. Hem shrugged and continued on.

On the fourth floor, Hem glanced over her right shoulder. Silvermist and Fira scurried behind a big potted fern.

On the second floor, Hem whirled around. "Hello?" she called. "Anyone there?"

Silvermist and Fira leaped into a dark corner. They held their breath and waited. Finally, Silvermist poked out her head. Hem was gone. "All clear," Silvermist whispered to Fira.

They flew quickly to the laundry room. But Hem had stopped suddenly just inside the door. They almost bumped into her. Thinking fast, Silvermist and Fira dived into a laundry basket.

"Lympia, did you hear something?" Hem asked a laundry talent fairy.

"Hmmm?" Lympia murmured. She wasn't paying attention. She was busy scrubbing leafkerchiefs in a washtub.

"I feel like somebody's following me," said Hem.

"Why would anyone follow you?" Lympia asked briskly. She handed Hem a pile of clean, neatly folded spiderwebs.

Hem shrugged.

Silvermist lifted her head out of the washing basket. Just then, a pile of dirty dresses tumbled down a laundry chute, landing on her.

"Oh!" she yelped.

"There! Did you hear that?" Hem demanded.

But Lympia had turned away and was already sprinkling fairy dust on a stained spider-silk tablecloth.

Holding the spiderwebs, Hem flew out of the room. Silvermist and Fira climbed quietly out of the basket, scattering dresses every which way.

"Tut, tut," they heard Lympia say as they hurried after Hem. "Tinker Bell needs to check these chutes. They're shooting clothes in all directions!"

Hem turned a corner.

Silvermist and Fira turned a corner.

Hem flew into the courtyard.

Silvermist and Fira flew into the court-yard.

Hem was flying faster and faster. She dropped a spiderweb, but she didn't bother to pick it up. She kept glancing behind her with a worried expression.

Silvermist and Fira flew faster and faster, too. They dodged the threads of spi-derweb Hem left in her wake. Silvermist watched for a dropped pin. But once again, she was out of luck.

Finally, Hem flew into the sewing room.

She slammed the door behind her – right in Silvermist's face.

"Quick! Through the window!" Fira whispered.

They flew out a window in the hall. They darted around the outside of the Home Tree and flew back in through a sewing-room window.

The workplace was abuzz with activity. Swiftly, Silvermist and Fira hid behind a wall tapestry. They were almost completely hidden. Only their feet stuck out from the bottom.

Silvermist peeked out from the side of the tapestry. One group of sewing talents sat in the middle of the floor. They were sorting pins into three piles: small, smaller, and smallest.

"I can't just pluck one from there," Silvermist whispered to Fira. "That wouldn't be finding it."

But then she spied something long and thin under a wicker chair in the corner. It was a pin! And she'd found it!

Hem was busy threading a needle. Everyone else was sewing and sorting. This was Silvermist's chance. She sneaked out from behind the tapestry. She stayed close to the wall. Quietly . . . calmly . . . she stooped to pick up the pin. Then she stood – and came face-to-face with Hem.

"Aha!" Hem cried. She whipped the tapestry away from the wall, revealing Fira. The rest of the sewing talents stopped working and looked up in surprise. "I knew something funny was going on," said Hem.

Fira stepped into the centre of the room. "Nothing funny is going on. We just wanted to . . . uh . . . watch you, Hem. Your talent is so extraordinary. What skill it takes to thread a pine needle! Why, I could never do that!"

"Well!" Hem said, relaxing a bit. She was flattered. "You can visit anytime, Fira."

"Really? We can visit anytime?" said Silvermist, smiling.

"We're very busy, preparing for the contest tomorrow," Hem said. She eyed Silvermist with concern. "Besides, we try to stay accident-free here. You know, with so many sharp pins and needles around."

Silvermist understood. Just like Dulcie, Hem didn't want Silvermist anywhere near her workspace. Silvermist turned to leave.

"Just a minute," Hem said. "What's that you're holding?"

"It's uh . . . uh . . . ," Silvermist tammered. "It's a pin." She opened her hand. "For luck."

Hem gave her a sad smile. "I wish I could help you, Silvermist. But we need every one of these pins to do our work."

Silvermist nodded. She walked over to the group of sorting fairies. She dropped the pin into the "smaller" pile.

"It's a 'smallest,'" Hem told her.

"Oh!" Silvermist bent to retrieve it.

"No, don't! I'll get it!" Hem cried. She lunged forward.

Startled, Silvermist jumped. She bumped into the piles of pins. Small, smaller, and smallest all scattered. They rolled under chairs, into cracks, and out of the door.

Silvermist whirled around. "Don't worry. I'll pick them up!" she cried.

"No! No! That's okay, Silvermist!" Hem said. "We'll take care of it."

Silvermist backed slowly out the door. In the hall, she tried to smile at Fira.

"That was a disaster," she said.

8

Fira led Silvermist outside. "Who needs a pin, anyway?" Fira said. "We have lots of other things on the good- luck list."

Fira took out the paper and read, "'Find the Circle Constellation in the night sky. The centre star winks once each night. When you see it wink, wish for luck.'"

"It's hours until sunset," Silvermist said. "What else?"

"'Find a swan feather.'"

"Hmmm." Silvermist thought out loud. "We'll have to find a swan first. I remember seeing a pair of swans swimming at Havendish Stream." She fluttered her wings. "Let's try that one!"

Havendish Stream was crowded with fairies and sparrow men. Some were washing their wings. Others picked flowers by the shore. But as they spotted Silvermist, they flew off one by one.

"Well, at least we have a clear view of the stream," Silvermist said. She was trying to look on the bright side.

The sparkling water and the sound of the waves lifted Silvermist's spirits. She flew from one end of the stream to the other. But she didn't spot a single swan.

She sighed. "The swans must have left. We'll have to try somewhere else. Somewhere outside Pixie Hollow." She looked at Fira. "This might take a while. Is that all right?"

Fira nodded. "I have to be back by dusk. The light talents are practicing a moonlight dance tonight. But it shouldn't take long to find one big swan."

The fairies set off. Silvermist hoped

Never Land's magic would help her. Maybe the wind would guide them in the right direction. Or maybe the island would shrink so they wouldn't have far to fly.

But if anything, the island seemed to grow. Their route seemed to get longer. It took hours just to reach Gull Pond, right outside Pixie Hollow.

Seagulls dived around the pond. But there were no swans.

So Silvermist and Fira flew even farther from Pixie Hollow, to Wough River. The river was wide. The water was high and noisy. They flew back and forth over it. Each time they crossed, Silvermist was sure the river had stretched even wider.

No, Never Land wasn't helping. And luck certainly wasn't on her side.

"No swans here," Silvermist said with a

sigh.

Finally, they came to Crescent Lake. They picked berries to snack on and sipped rainwater cupped in leaves.

Fira looked at the sun. "It's getting late. If we don't see a swan soon, we'll have to turn back."

"Look!" Silvermist cried. She pointed to the sky. "There are two now."

The swans flew past a nest built on the bank.

"Come on!" Fira took Silvermist by the hand. "Let's check there!"

The fairies landed in the nest, which was made from grass and twigs. They flitted from one end to the other, searching for a feather.

"No." Silvermist shook her head. "There aren't any here."

"That's okay." Fira flapped her wings

harder. "We'll follow the swans, like we followed Hem. They're bound to lose at least
one feather!"

Silvermist started to follow Fira. But
something jerked her back. She turned and
saw that her dress was caught on a twig. She
twisted to try to free herself. But the cloth
was stuck tight. Of all the luck!

She heard a flutter of wings behind her.
"Fira!" she called. "Come closer and—"

Silvermist turned, expecting to see Fira
hovering next to her. Instead, she came face-
to-eyeball with an enormous angry black
swan.

"Oh!" Silvermist's heart beat fast.

The swan stared at her. Its beak was
inches from her face. Clearly, it didn't like
having a little fairy in its nest.

"Calm down," Silvermist said to herself. "Swans are beautiful, gentle

creatures."

But this swan was huge and seemed menacing. Silvermist's heart was racing now. She grabbed her dress and pulled hard.

Rrrip! Silvermist's dress tore free.

Moments later, she and Fira hovered behind a tree, hidden from the swan. Silvermist took a deep breath. "That was close."

The swan had joined its mate. Now they both circled lazily over the water. From a safe distance, they seemed lovely and majestic once again.

"Should we follow them?" Fira asked.

Silvermist shook her head. She'd had enough of swans for one day. Besides, the sun was low in the sky. The fairies had missed lunch and dinner.

"We should leave now," she told Fira. "Before it gets too late."

"You're right," Fira said. "I'm tired."

"Me too," Silvermist agreed quickly. Their fairy dust was wearing off. Her wings felt heavy, and they still had to fly home. It wasn't fair to make Fira keep searching, Silvermist thought.

As the fairies headed back to Pixie Hollow, the low sun vanished behind the trees. Fira turned up her glow. But it was still hard to see.

"Is this the way?" Silvermist asked. She flew into a small thicket.

Fira struggled to shine more brightly. She squinted. "No!" she called. "That's the—"

Silvermist flew out of the bramble. She scratched her arms. "I know, I know. That's the patch of itchy ivy we passed earlier."

Silvermist was tired and uncomfortable. Her dress was dirty and torn. She flew the rest of the way home in silence.

Will I be doomed forever? she wondered. *And what if the curse gets worse?*

She had no idea what would happen next. She wanted to be the old calm, cool Silvermist everyone counted on. But how could she be when she was cursed?

When they reached the Home Tree entrance, Silvermist hugged Fira tightly. "At least you're back in time for your light practice," she told her friend. "And now that I know where the swans are, I can find a feather in the morning. Of course," she added, "I won't get so close next time!"

There! Just having a plan made Silvermist feel hopeful.

"Swan feathers?" Beck flew into the Home Tree as Fira flew out. She paused next to Silvermist. "I'm afraid you won't have any luck with that. It's not the moulting season. Swans won't lose their feathers for

Hi Guys!

My fairy friends and I are fully in tune with the nature of Pixie Hollow. There are so many different types of colourful plants, flowers and trees, all of which change and flower as the seasons alter . . .

In Pixie Hollow, all the seasons co-exist together. It's truly a **miracle of nature**. The sun shines in one part, where trees are in **full bloom** and the vines bear fruit. In another, the trees are changing colour and an autumn nip is in the air. Elsewhere, snow covers the ground and icicles hang from the windowsills. Then there's another area where the flowers are pushing anew out of the earth. This means us fairies can always choose what kind of weather we want to experience.

No matter what the weather's like, the **fairies adore all of the different seasons!**

Spring and Summer in Pixie Hollow

It's the job of the Nature Talent Fairies to change the seasons on the mainland and as the winter draws to an end, the garden fairies fly out of Pixie Hollow to plant the seeds of spring. Only then do the winter days start to fade away, and spring takes over.

Spring and Summer are marked in Pixie Hollow by the long, warm, hazy days. Fairies love being outside, and spring is when the **pretty wildflowers** start pushing their way through the soil after the cold winters. By summer, Pixie Hollow is ablaze with rainbow coloured flowers, and their delightful scent fills the air.

Fairy Clothes

As the weather grows warmer, the fairies are able to wear their summer finery. They put on their cool violet petal *sundresses*, sunflower petal *bonnets* and prettiest *sandals*, which they weave out of grasses. Some of the sandals have heels as thin as pine needles. They accessorize with **pretty acorn bags** and **ivy leaf belts**.

How Fairies Celebrate the Season

The most playful fairies adore **spring** and **summer**, because there are so many fun games to play. There are *dragonflies* to be chased, *rainbows* to be spun and *ladybirds* to be painted. Out in the meadows they have races on the backs of mice and birds, or enjoy a game of fairy tag.

On the longest day of the year, the fairies hold a Midsummer Ball, where they dress up in their most **beautiful ball gowns** and dance the night away.

Autumn in Pixie Hollow

The colours of autumn are extra **vivid** when they're dusted with a bit of *Pixie Hollow magic*. The leaves begin changing from green to amber, gold and scarlet. The garden fairies are kept extra busy keeping things tidy when the leaves start to fall from the trees! The garden fairies also have other jobs to do, like pruning bushes and trees.

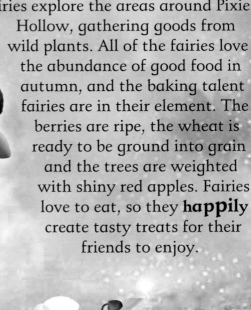

The harvester fairies explore the areas around Pixie Hollow, gathering goods from wild plants. All of the fairies love the abundance of good food in autumn, and the baking talent fairies are in their element. The berries are ripe, the wheat is ready to be ground into grain and the trees are weighted with shiny red apples. Fairies love to eat, so they **happily** create tasty treats for their friends to enjoy.

Fairy Clothes

Autumn is a time when the fairies wear slightly thicker clothes, as the weather is starting to get cooler. They dress in darker colours, such as purples, oranges and deep reds. The fairies weave headdresses out of corn and crab apples, and wear *beautiful* dresses made of marigolds and roses. Moss is in abundance, which makes the softest trousers and slippers.

How Fairies Celebrate the Season

Autumn means it's harvest time, and the fairies have their harvest festival. This is a time where the fairies show their thanks to nature for the gifts they've been given – not just food, but for the flowers, plants and trees too. The fairies are very appreciative of nature as they couldn't live without its food to eat, its *flower petals*, which provide clothes to wear, and its twigs and grasses that make the houses and provide shelter. They celebrate with *pumpkin pies*, freshly baked breads and freshly squeezed *apple juices*.

Winter in Pixie Hollow

A gentle dusting of snow covers Pixie Hollow during the winter months. Delicate lacy frost decorates the windows in pretty patterns, and everywhere looks breathtakingly beautiful. Most of the plants and trees are resting, ready for spring and their new burst of growth, so the garden fairies get a well-earned rest.

The fairies huddle in each other's houses, keeping warm in front of **crackling fires**. They play games together, such as hunt the acorn and roll the conker. Other times they make clothes, bake, or simply chatter and laugh together.

Fairy Clothes

Fairies don't like to be cold, so they wrap up warm during winter in Pixie Hollow. They wear cosy jumpers knitted from *dandelion fluff*, thick layers of skirts woven from ivy and wrap up with moss mufflers and gloves made from tightly coiled ferns. They put on sturdy boots, woven with spaghetti laces, to make sure they don't slip on the ice.

The fairies often carry *flower petal umbrellas* with them, to protect them from dripping water on the trees, or unexpected snowfalls.

How Fairies Celebrate the Season

The fairies decorate their houses during the winter season, to keep things **bright** and **cheerful** while the nights are drawing in. They have decorations made out of holly berries and fir cones.

When the nearby lagoon freezes over, the fairies can go *skating*. They also like to go *sledging* on tiny *toboggans* made out of tree bark. Another fun winter game the fairies enjoy is *snowball fights* – but the fairies play up in the air! The snowballs fly everywhere, and they have be extra fast to avoid getting hit.

Take the Fairy Seasons Test!

Which is your perfect season?
Take the test below to find out

1.   What is your favourite kind of weather?
A.   Warm sunshine
B.   Cool, with a refreshing breeze
C.   Windy days, where the leaves dance around you
D.   Snow and frost

2.   What is your favourite kind of activity?
A.   Relaxing in the garden with a good book
B.   Gardening, such as planting bulbs and flowers
C.   Flying a kite
D.   Curling up by a fire with a cup of hot chocolate

3.   When are you at your happiest?
A.   When you're playing outside
B.   When you're watching things grow
C.   When you're collecting beautiful coloured leaves
      for art projects
D.   When you're having a snowball fight

Answers:
- *If you scored mostly As then your perfect season is summer.*
- *If you scored mostly Bs then your perfect season is spring.*
- *If you scored mostly Cs then your perfect season is autumn.*
- *If you scored mostly Ds then your perfect season is winter.*

months and months."

All that trouble for nothing! thought Silvermist. And now she didn't have a plan after all. What if she was cursed forever?

9

FIRA HAD GONE to light-talent practice. Beck had gone to her room. Pixie Hollow was quiet. Silvermist stood by the Home Tree, unsure of what to do.

If she went to sleep, would she fall out of bed and break a wing? If she flew to the dairy barn, would she turn the milk sour? If she went to the fairy-dust mill, would the dust blow away with the wind?

Would disaster follow anywhere she went?

The waterball contest was early in the morning. If she wanted to be in it – if she wanted to end her streak of bad luck – she had to keep searching. She had to find good luck somewhere.

She scratched one itchy elbow, then the other. Then she looked up at the night sky.

The night sky! She could search for the Circle Constellation.

Slowly and carefully, she made her way to the Never Land beach. Here, she had the soothing sounds of the waves and the greatest view of the stars.

Silvermist shivered. The night air was chilly. She found a leaf to wrap herself in. Then she settled against a rock and tilted her chin up to the sky.

Bright lights dotted the darkness.

Silvermist had never really paid attention to the stars before. But now she could see that they grouped together in patterns that almost made pictures.

Do they always look like this? she wondered. Something seemed different. Then she realized that the constellations were changing shape.

She thought she spied the Circle Constellation, but it changed into a square. An arrow shape turned into a snake. A leaf turned into a feather.

Was that how the stars always were?

Maybe her eyes were fooling her. Or maybe this was more bad luck. Were the stars playing tricks, just the way the Wough River had been when it had widened as she'd tried to cross it?

Silvermist felt more determined than ever. She could wait until the stars tired of their game. She'd be patient. She was good at that.

Minutes ticked by. Silvermist kept staring at the sky. Her eyes began to ache from the strain. She was afraid to blink, afraid she'd miss the winking star. Still, she waited.

Suddenly, the stars froze in place. Silvermist leaped to her feet. There, to the left, was the Circle Constellation. She was sure of it. Right in the middle was one star. The star that would wink.

Silvermist held her breath. Would it happen now?

Yes! The star flashed once, off and on. She squeezed her eyes shut and said, "I wish for all my bad luck to end."

She opened her eyes and sighed with relief. She'd done it. She'd reversed the curse.

Now the stars were moving once again.

They floated closer to the ground, and closer still.

All at once, Silvermist understood. The bright lights weren't stars at all. They were light-talent fairies practicing their dance.

"That's what confused me." For a moment, Silvermist closed her eyes and pictured the changing shapes. "I guess I just wanted to believe so much . . ."

er voice trailed off. She didn't have the strength to finish the sentence. A lone tear fell from her eye, then another and another. Soon Silvermist's tears flowed faster and faster.

Silvermist – the water-talent fairy who hardly ever cried – was sobbing.

Silvermist spent that night alone on the beach. She was afraid to go back to her room. With all those clouds in the sky, a storm could be brewing. She didn't want to attract the storm to the Home Tree.

If anything happened here at the beach, she'd be the only one in danger.

She slept fitfully. She meant to wake up early to search for another good-luck charm. Even though finding one seemed impossible, she wanted to keep trying. But her deepest sleep came after sunrise. And she was so tired from flying and searching. She didn't stir until she heard a voice.

"Good morning, darling."

Silvermist opened her eyes. Vidia was sitting next to her on the sand.

"You seem to have overslept," Vidia continued. "Good thing I decided to be your own personal wake-up fairy. I would never want you to miss an important event like the waterball contest."

Silvermist sat up. She rubbed her eyes.

"The tournament begins in ten minutes, sweetie. Everyone is expecting you," said Vidia.

"I don't think anyone wants me there. Fairies fly in the other direction when they see me coming now."

"That may be. Really, who could blame them?" Vidia paused. "But Queen Clarion announced at breakfast that she expects the game to go on as planned, with you playing, darling. It seems she wants life in Pixie Hollow to continue as if nothing's changed."

Silvermist took a deep breath. If Queen Clarion needed her to be there, she'd be there. Besides, she had told everyone she'd be in the contest. And she always kept her word.

"I'm ready," she said.

"Good." Vidia brushed the sand from her leggings. "This is one event I wouldn't want to miss."

BY THE TIME Silvermist got to the contest field, everything was already in place. Hem and the other sewing talents had finished a beautiful new gown for Queen Clarion. Celebration-setup fairies had carefully moved the spiderweb target to one end of the field. And fairies from all talents had come to watch.

Queen Clarion sat on a large colourful mat near the targets. The other fairies and sparrow men milled about, talking and laughing.

As Silvermist walked past, Hem drew in her breath. "She's here," Hem hissed to another sewing talent. "Hold on to your pins!"

Heads turned. Wings fluttered. One by one, the fairies edged away from Silvermist.

But Fira made her way over. "It will be okay," she told her friend. "Maybe your luck is turning."

"I don't think so," Silvermist said quietly. On the way to the contest, she'd picked up a leftover muffin from the tearoom. Before she could take one bite, she'd dropped it in a muddy puddle.

"Fairies and sparrow men!" Queen Clarion said, clapping her hands. The crowd quietened. "Water talents, take your places behind the marked line. Everyone else, be seated. The competition is about to begin!"

Fira hurried off to join the other light talents. Silvermist walked slowly towards the water fairies, who were forming a line. Maybe no one would notice her if she stayed at the back.

Queen Clarion reminded everyone of the rules. "Each water talent will get five tries to hit the target. Those who do best will go on to the next set of targets."

Rani stood at a line drawn in the dirt. She stared at the spiderweb target and the bull's-eye circle in its centre. Then she dipped her hand into a bucket of water. She patted the water into a smooth ball. Winding up her arm, she pitched the water-ball at the target.

The ball hit the spiderweb, close to the bull's-eye. The crowd cheered.

Water-talent after water-talent tried the game, until only Silvermist was left.

Hesitantly, she stepped forward. She scooped up the water, then stole a glance at Vidia. Silvermist wound up and made the throw.

The waterball soared through the air. It went up, up, up, then down, down, down.

Silvermist held her breath. The waterball

was going towards the target. It was heading right for it. It was going to hit –

The waterball hit Queen Clarion full in the face.

Everyone gasped. Queen Clarion was soaked from head to toe. Water dripped from her hair and her dress. A puddle formed by her feet. Helper fairies hurried over with moss towels.

Silvermist could barely look. What had she done? And what would the queen do now?

To Silvermist's amazement, Queen Clarion . . . laughed!

"Well, that cooled me off!" said the queen. She wrung out her hair. Water drops flew everywhere, sprinkling the nearby fairies.

The queen laughed harder. Then Prilla clapped her hands and giggled. Tinker Bell chuckled. Soon everyone was laughing – everyone but Silvermist.

Queen Clarion took off one shoe and turned it over. A stream of water poured out.

Finally, Silvermist began to laugh. And the longer she laughed, the harder she laughed. Queen Clarion pouring water out of her shoe! The idea of it!

"Oh, oh." Silvermist laughed so hard her stomach hurt. She bent over, her arms hugging her sides.

And then she saw a five-leaf clover, right by her feet. A lucky clover.

"Rosetta!" Silvermist called. "Come see this! Fira! Tink! Everyone! Look!"

Fairies crowded around Silvermist. The clover was beautiful, slender but strong. Silvermist felt stronger too. Finally, she'd found a good-luck charm.

"Is it all right to pick it?" she asked.

Iris rushed over, her plant book already open. "'Five-leaf clovers are meant to be picked,'" she read out loud. "'Their magic keeps them alive forever.'"

"They're magic – and lucky!" Fira added.

Gently, Silvermist tugged the clover from the ground. She held it in her hand, examining it carefully.

"This isn't a flower show," Vidia said with a yawn. "It's still your turn, Silvermist."

The contest! Silvermist had forgotten all about it. She tucked the clover behind her ear.

"Don't get rattled now, darling," Vidia called from her seat on a branch. Her voice was syrupy. "Finding a clover is all well and good. But how can it compete with a powerful curse?"

Silvermist gazed steadily at Vidia. *Rattled*, she thought. *That's exactly what Vidia wants me to be. Ever since Vidia fell in the water, she's wanted to get back at me. Every chance she's got, she's tried to upset me.*

So was that what the accidents had been about? Not a curse . . . or even bad luck. Just Silvermist making mistakes because she had felt flustered and unsure?

I don't know! she thought. But did it matter?

For the first time in a long while, Silvermist was thinking clearly. And that was when she remembered something else – the seashell she'd lost, the one she'd thought had fallen out of her dress.

She remembered now. She'd put it in the fold at her waist. She put her hand in that fold of her dress. And there it was! The special seashell.

"Take your time, Silvermist." Vidia tossed her hair. "It's not as if anyone's waiting."

"I was just thinking," Silvermist said in her old calm way. "And now, before I throw the ball, I have something to say."

The fairies and sparrow men gazed at her intently.

"I'm not sure if I had bad luck or just a few bad days. I'm not sure about these old superstitions at all. But there is one thing I do know. If you believe you'll have bad luck, then you'll have bad luck."

That was why it didn't make a difference if the curse was real or all in her mind.

Silvermist turned to leave the contest. She didn't care about winning or losing or proving anything to anybody.

"Poor, sweet Silvermist," Vidia said.

"She can't go on. She's lost her nerve."

Well, thought Silvermist, *maybe I have to prove something to* one *fast-flying fairy.*

She turned her back to the target. Then she tossed the waterball over her shoulder. It soared through the air. Silvermist heard it hit and splash all over. All around her, fairies gasped in shock.

"Bull's-eye!" cried Fira.

Silvermist grinned. Had that been a lucky shot? She didn't know. And she didn't care.

A
Masterpiece
for
Bess

WRITTEN BY
Lara Bergen

ILLUSTRATED BY
The Disney Storybook Artists

1

"EVERYBODY! COME TO MY room!"

Tinker Bell flew about the tearoom. In a silvery voice she called out to the fairies and sparrow men gathered around the tables.

Lily and Rosetta, two garden-talent fairies, looked up from their breakfast of elderberry scones.

"What's the hurry, Tink?" asked Lily.

"Bess has just painted my portrait – and you've got to come and see it!" Tinker

Bell urged.

Rosetta and Lily looked at each other in surprise. It wasn't every day that Bess painted a new portrait! What was the occasion? they wondered. But before they could ask, Tink had darted out of the tearoom door and into the kitchen.

"Let's go," Rosetta said to Lily. They followed Tink through the Home Tree up to her room.

There the fairies packed themselves in wing to wing, like honeybees in a hive. They could see Bess, in her usual paint splattered skirt, standing at the front of the room. She was hanging a life-size, five-inch painting of Tinker Bell.

"Isn't it amazing?" gushed Tink. She flew up behind Lily and Rosetta and landed with a bounce on her loaf-pan bed.

And indeed it was. Bess's painting was so lifelike, if a fairy hadn't known better, she might have thought there were *two* Tinks in the room. No detail – from the dimples in Tink's cheeks to her woven sweetgrass belt – was overlooked. What Tink loved most about the painting, though, were the gleaming metal objects piled all around her: pots, pans, kettles, and colanders. She felt as if she could almost pull each one out of the painting.

It was a perfect portrait, as everyone could see. Right away the oohs and aahs began to echo off the tin walls of Tink's room. Her lemon yellow glow turned slightly tangerine as she blushed. As Pixie Hollow's busiest painter, she was used to praise. But she never tired of hearing it.

"It's just what Tink's room needed," added Gwinn, a decoration-talent fairy. She gazed around Tink's metal-filled room.

"What's the occasion?" asked Rosetta.

"Oh, no occasion, really," said Bess. She brushed her long brown fringe out of her violet eyes. "Tink fixed my best palette knife, and I wanted to do something nice in return."

All around her, the fairies murmured approvingly. Bess felt her heart swell with pride. *This is what art is all about,* she thought. Times like these made her work worthwhile.

"Personally, I don't see what the fuss is for," a thorny voice said above the din. "Honestly, my little darlings, what's so great about a fairy standing still?"

Bess didn't have to turn around. She knew who the voice belonged to – and so did everybody else. Vidia, the fastest – and by far the meanest – of the fast-flying-talent fairies, came forward.

"Oh, Vidia," Tink said with a groan. "You wouldn't know fine art if it flew up and nipped you on the nose."

"Yeah, don't listen to her, Bess," Gwinn called out.

"It's okay," Bess assured them. "Every fairy is welcome to have her own opinion."

But as she looked at the portrait again, she frowned slightly. It wasn't that Vidia's criticism bothered her. She'd learned long ago to let the spiteful fairy's snide comments roll off her wings like dewdrops. But Vidia's remark had started the wheels in Bess's mind turning.

"You know… ," Bess began.

She searched the room for Vidia. But the fairy had already flown away.

"'You know' what?" asked Tink.

Bess shook her head. She turned to Tink with a sunny grin. "There's a whole day ahead of us!" she said. "I don't know about you fairies, but I've got work to do."

Spreading her wings, she lifted into the air. "Thanks for coming, everyone," she called.

And with a happy wave, Bess zipped off to her studio.

2

NOWHERE ELSE DID Bess feel as content as she did in her studio.

Most of the art-talent fairies had studios in the lower branches of the Home Tree. But to Bess there never seemed to be quite enough light – or privacy – there to get her work done. Instead, she had made her studio in an old wooden tangerine crate that had washed up onto a shore of Never Land. She had moved the crate (using magic, of course) to the sunniest, most peaceful corner of Pixie Hollow. It had been her home away from home ever since.

Over time, she'd added things to the crate: a birch-bark cabinet to keep her canvases dry, a soapstone sink in which to wash her brushes, and even a twig bed with a thick hummingbird-down quilt to sleep on when she was painting late into the night.

Bess's studio had grown more and more cluttered. It was, in fact, a bit of a mess. She was not one for tidying up. Why put things away, she always wondered, when you were sure to have to pull them out again someday?

As soon as she reached her studio, Bess began to mix her paints. She took a jar of fragrant linseed oil down from a shelf. Next she brought out a gleaming cherrywood box. The box was polished to a mirrorlike shine. Bess's name was carved into the lid. A carpenter-talent fairy had given it to her as a gift many years before. It was still one of her most prized possessions.

Bess lifted the top of the box. She looked down at the rainbow of powdered pigments inside. Of all the things in her studio, these were the ones she treated like gold.

"Hmm," she mused out loud. "Which colours should I mix first? Orange? Indigo? Hmm... What is that *smell*?"

Following her nose, Bess turned to find two brown eyes peeking in at her through the slats in the tangerine crate.

"Dulcie?" she said in suprise. "Is that you?"

Visitors to her studio were rare. Bess fumbled with the latch as she opened the door. "What is it?"

"Oh, nothing," said Dulcie sweetly. "I was just passing through the orchard and thought I'd say hi. Oh! And I thought you might like some poppy puff rolls. Fresh out of the oven!"

Dulcie grinned and held up a basket. She lifted a checked linen cloth off the top. The rich scents of butter and tarragon filled Bess's nose. Her mouth began to water.

"Goodness, Dulcie – your famous rolls.

You're really too kind!" said Bess, more surprised than ever.

"I thought you'd be hungry," said Dulcie, handing one to Bess. "Especially after working so hard on Tinker Bell's portrait."

Bess took a bite. *"Mmm,"* she said. She closed her eyes and let the flaky layers melt on her tongue. "Delicious, Dulcie! This is so unexpected – and very nice of you! If there's anything I can do for you, just let me know."

"Well," replied Dulcie, "if you wanted to do a portrait of me, that would be fine! I guess I could even pose for you right now. Why, I could pose with my rolls! What do you think? Should I carry the whole basket or just cradle one in my hand like this?"

Bess swallowed what was left of her roll in one surprised gulp.

"Um… uh… actually," she stammered, "I was just about to… "

"I know!" Dulcie exclaimed. "I'll hold a roll in one hand, and the basket in the other! There! Are you getting this, Bess?"

Bess wiped her buttery hands on her skirt. She hadn't planned to paint another portrait. But how could she refuse? And it certainly was flattering to have such an eager model.

"Okay," Bess said. "Why not? I just need to mix up some paints and pick out my brushes."

Dulcie positively fluttered with glee.

From her box, Bess pulled out jars, each filled with a different colour of paint powder: green, blue, black, gold. She decided to start with the chestnut powder, which was remarkably close to the shade of Dulcie's hair. She poured a small mound onto a piece of glass and added linseed oil. Then she carefully used her palette knife to fold the two together. Soon she had a smooth chocolaty brown paste.

She mixed a few more colours and scooped them onto her palette. Pleased, she pulled a clean paintbrush from her pocket. Then she took a hard look at her model. Bess frowned.

"Dulcie," she said, "I wonder if maybe you could move around a little."

"Move around?" said Dulcie. "But what if I drop my rolls?"

And just then, a knock sounded at the door.

3

BESS OPENED HER DOOR to find an enormous bouquet of flowers. Two dainty feet in violet-petal shoes poked out below.

"Rosetta? Is that you?" Bess asked.

"Yes, it's me," replied a muffled voice from behind the flowers. Rosetta's pretty face peeked out from the side. "I brought you these," she said. With a groan, she heaved the heavy bunch towards Bess.

"Lily of the valley. My favourite! What a nice surprise, Rosetta!" Bess exclaimed.

Bess managed to drop the flowers into her cockleshell umbrella stand. She knocked over a few paint pots and canvases as she did.

"I thought you'd like them." Rosetta beamed. "In fact, I thought you might enjoy *painting* them. Or perhaps it would be better for you if I posed *with* them! As if I were walking through my garden, you know? Something like this – "

Pointing her nose in the air, Rosetta rose on one toe and struck a dramatic pose. "Luckily, I just had my hair done. Usually it's such a mess. Make sure you get each curl, now. Oh, this is going to look so great in my room!"

Bess was speechless. "Er… "

"What Bess is trying to say," Dulcie called from across the room, "is that we are already in the middle of a painting." She held up her basket of rolls for Rosetta to see. "As we say in the kitchen, 'First fairy to come, first fairy served!' But don't worry. Bess will let you know when she's done with *my* portrait. Won't you, Bess?"

"Er… ," said Bess.

"Oh, I see," Rosetta said. Her delicate wings slumped sadly. "Well, in the meantime, I'll go clear a space back in my room for my new portrait. I know exactly where it should go!" She gave them both a little wave and hurried out.

"Fly safely!" called Dulcie.

Bess closed the door behind Rosetta. She felt extremely flattered – and still a little stunned. It was part of her role as an art talent to do paintings for her fellow fairies. Till that morning, they had always been for special occasions: an Arrival Day portrait, or a new painting for the Home Tree corridor. In between, she was as free as a bird to paint whatever she wanted.

But now, right out of the blue, *two* fairies wanted their pictures painted in one day! That was a record for any art-talent fairy, Bess was sure.

Bless my wings, she thought. *Who knew that Never fairies had such great taste!*

"Shall we continue?" asked Dulcie.

Bess picked up her brush and nodded. "Of course!"

But within minutes, another knock sounded at the door... then another... and another!

By midday, fifteen fairies had paid Bess a visit, and fourteen wanted their portraits painted. (Terence, a dust-talent sparrow man, had stopped by only to drop off Bess's daily portion of fairy dust and to compliment her on Tinker Bell's portrait.)

Everyone wanted a portrait just like Tink's. There were so many requests, in fact, that Bess had given up on painting them one at a time. Instead, she had each fairy come in to sit for a sketch. Her plan was to finish the paintings later. But by the fourteenth fairy, even finishing a sketch began to look iffy.

"Fern, it's really hard to sketch you when you keep dusting my paper," Bess said to the dusting-talent fairy hovering over her easel.

"Oops!" said Fern. She darted back to the pedestal Bess had set up for her. "It's a habit," she explained. "But *really,* Bess." She shook her head. "I do wish you'd let a dusting talent in here once in a while! How can you stand it? And now, with all these baskets and flowers... my goodness! It's a forest of dust-catchers!"

It was true. Bess's studio was even more cluttered than usual. Fairies who'd come hoping for portraits had brought gifts. There were berries and walnuts from the harvest-talent fairies, cheeses from the dairy-talent fairies, and baskets upon baskets of goodies from the talents in the kitchen. Then there were more baskets from the grass-weaving talents. Not to mention a bubbling foot-high fountain from Silvermist, the water-talent fairy.

Luckily, not all fairies had come with gifts. Hairdressing, floor-polishing, and window- and wing-washing fairies had come offering their services. One music-talent fairy even played a song she'd written just for Bess. (To Bess's dismay, it was *still* stuck in her head!)

"Oh!" Fern exclaimed suddenly. "There's a speck on your pencil there! Hold on!" She examined it. "Looks like pollen." Then another grain caught her eye. "Over there by the door! Fairy dust. I'll bet Terence left that one."

Feather duster waving at full speed, Fern darted about the room. Bess tried her best to sketch the fairy in action.

At least this is the last sketch I have to do, Bess told herself. *Then just fourteen portraits to paint...*

Knock-knock-knock.

Bess's stomach did a backflip. *Again?* For a second, she was tempted to pretend that no one was home. But she quickly realized that Fern's darting glow and humming duster had already given them away.

Slowly, Bess opened the door.

"Oh, Quill! It's you!" Bess let out a sigh of relief that even Fern could hear. "You wouldn't believe how many fairies and sparrow men have come to my studio today," she said.

She tried not to sound boastful. But she wanted Quill to know how much the other fairies liked her work. Bess always felt self-conscious around Quill. Perhaps it was because Quill was so unbelievably neat, while Bess was so messy.

"Fourteen!" Bess blurted, unable to hold back. "Everyone wanting portraits! I've never seen anything like it!" she went on. "I mean, just look at all the things they've brought me!" She waved her brush at the piles of gifts. Then suddenly she paused.

"You weren't coming to ask for a portrait, too, were you?"

The art-talent fairy shook her head and smiled. "No, I just came by to see if you were ready to go to lunch. I've heard they're serving mushroom tarts and buttercup soup!"

Buttercup soup! Bess hadn't had that in ages, it seemed. *Mmm* – she could taste it already. Then her eyes fell on the pile of sketches on her table.

"I can't." She sighed. "Everyone is counting on me to finish the portraits as soon as I can. I've never seen fairies so passionate about art." She glanced at Quill out of the corner of her eye. "My portrait of Tinker Bell really touched them. *Deeply!* Mushroom tarts and buttercup soup will simply have to wait."

Bess sighed again. "It's hard to be so important. But I am up to the challenge – and I won't let Pixie Hollow down! Please give the other art talents my greetings, though, won't you, Quill?"

Quill was about to respond when Fern suddenly poked her head out from behind the birch-bark cabinet.

"Did you say buttercup soup?" she asked. "Hang on, Quill. I'm coming with you!"

She flew across the room, swiping at a few dust grains along the way. "Let me know when my portrait's done, Bess. Oooh! I cannot wait to dust it!" she said brightly.

Bess watched the fairies go, and she shut the door behind them. She looked at the sketch she had *tried* to do of Fern. It wasn't perfect, but it was fine for a sketch, she decided. *And it's probably a good idea to start painting now*, Bess thought. *I have a lot to do!*

Filled with a sense of duty, Bess churned

out several portraits in the next few hours. But when she started the portrait of Rosetta, the garden-talent fairy – who had *insisted* on wearing her best rose-petal outfit – Bess froze.

Oh, no!

She couldn't believe it. She was all out of red paint! She couldn't finish Rosetta's portrait without it!

There was just one thing to do: go out and get more. This emergency called for berry juice – and lots of it.

Bess picked up a piece of paper and one of her best calligraphy twigs. She wrote a sign and hung it on her door:

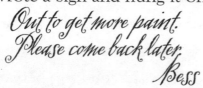

Out to get more paint.
Please come back later.
Bess

Then she grabbed one of Dulcie's rolls, along with the first basket she could find, and flew out into the warm afternoon.

4

THE CURRANT ORCHARD was not far from Bess's studio. It was just across Havendish Stream.

Currant juice was a cheerful bright red, which would make fine paint, Bess knew. As she flew towards the fruits, they looked so pretty that Bess had an urge to paint them right then and there. Ah, but how could she? So many fairies were waiting for their portraits. She couldn't disappoint them.

Bess flitted from branch to branch. She piled as many plump currants into her basket as she could carry. A basketful would be – she hoped – enough for now.

She placed one last fruit atop her wobbly pile, then reached out and picked one for herself. If she couldn't paint the currants, at least she could taste them!

She licked her lips, then took a big

hungry bite. The sweet red juice dribbled down her chin. Bess watched it fall, drip by drip, onto her skirt. It mixed with paint splatters there.

She swiped at her chin with the back of her hand. *Yes!* she thought with satisfaction. *This colour will do just fine!*

When she had finished eating, Bess grabbed hold of the basket's handle. She stretched up her wings, ready to fly away. The heavy basket, however, was not going anywhere. Bess could pick it up – just barely. But she couldn't carry it more than an inch at a time.

She tried unloading a few currants, but it didn't help much. And if she took out too many, she wouldn't have enough to make paint when she got home.

Enviously, Bess watched a bluebird soaring overhead. If only she could speak to animals like an animal-talent fairy, maybe she could get some help. But she couldn't even tell the gnats hovering around to go away. No matter how hard she shooed, they just kept returning.

"Oh, well," Bess said with a sigh. "I guess an inch at a time will have to do."

Bess flew – or hopped, really – out of the orchard and back towards her studio. By the time she reached Havendish Stream, she had settled into a comfortable rhythm: *flap, flap, flap, flap-jump-land. Flap, flap, flap, flap-jump-land.* But the crystal-clear stream stopped her short.

It wasn't that Havendish Stream was very big; a young deer could have crossed it in a single leap. To a fairy, however, it was huge. And there wasn't a bridge. Fairies usually just flew over the stream.

What am I going to do now? thought Bess. The stream was too wide to hop across. And though   she   didn't   mind getting her feet and legs wet, she didn't want to risk getting her wings wet, too. Water soaked into fairy wings, as into a sponge. And if the stream was deep enough, waterlogged wings could drag her under.

Still, Bess had got this far. She wasn't going to give up now!

She thought for a moment. Then she picked up one of the plump currants. With a mighty heave, she tossed it across the stream. The currant landed with a soft bounce on the moss on the other side.

Bess cheered, then reached for another. Soon she was tossing currants across the stream one after the other.

When her basket was empty, Bess lifted it effortlessly and flew across the stream. Then she refilled it and set off hopping once more. She was quite pleased with her clever solution.

"Now to make some paint!"

Back at her studio, Bess dragged a well-worn coconut shell from its resting place against her crate. She set it on the grass next to the back wall and dumped her basketful of currants into it.

Normally, Bess made her paints in small batches. But she'd spent far more time collecting the currants than she'd planned. If she was ever going to get all those fairies their portraits, she'd have to start speeding things up – a lot! That meant making *lots* of paint.

Bess kicked off her shoes and rolled up her spider-silk leggings. Then, ever so carefully, she climbed into the shell.

"Oops!" Bess slipped and almost fell. She caught herself on the shell.

POP! Squish! The pulpy fruit burst out of its skin and oozed coolly between her toes. Bess stomped around in the bowl. Her feet moved faster and faster.

She tried her best to keep her wings high and dry. But she could tell they were growing heavy with juice. *No matter,* she thought. *They'll have plenty of time to dry while I paint.* She looked down at the ruby red juice in the shell. Her heart filled with joy. Without thinking about it, she began to sing...

"Oh, fairy, fairy, fly with me – "

"Bess? What are you doing?"

The voice behind Bess took her by surprise. She wavered, and her foot slipped.

Splash!

Bess fell face-first into the sticky red currant mash.

"Bess?"

Slowly, Bess reached for the edge of the shell and pulled herself up. Peeking over the side, she saw Quill's pretty face staring back. In Quill's hands was a tray full of dishes covered with acorn caps.

"Are you all right?" Quill asked.

"Perfectly fine," said Bess. She spat out a bit of currant. "I'm just – uh – making some paint for all my portraits."

Inwardly, Bess groaned. Why did Quill always catch her in her messiest moment?

With as much dignity as she could manage, Bess pulled herself out of the shell. She tumbled to the ground. Covered in bright red juice, she looked as if she had a very bad sunburn.

"I brought you some dinner," Quill said. She set down the tray. "You need a hot meal to keep up your strength."

Even through the currant juice, Bess could smell the rich scents coming from the dishes. She wished, more than anything, that Quill hadn't seen her this way. But it was hard not to be grateful for such a kind gesture.

"I know I'll enjoy it," Bess said.

"Would you like some help washing

your wings?" Quill asked. Her tone was sincere. But Bess caught the corners of her mouth turning up in a smile.

Bess shook her head and blushed. "Oh, no," she assured Quill. "I'll get to that... when I can."

"As you wish," Quill replied. She fluttered her wings and turned back towards the Home Tree.

5

DESPITE HER EMBARRASSMENT, Bess enjoyed the dinner Quill had brought. And she hoped it would give her more energy to work.

But painting wasn't easy. The currant juice quickly dried into a sticky sap. It made Bess's hair and clothes stiff and her wings all but useless.

If I'm ever going to get more painting done, Bess thought, *I'll have to clean myself up.*

She set off towards Havendish Stream again. Her wings were too stiff now for her even to hop, so instead she walked through the meadow. Unfortunately, because fairies hardly ever walked, there were no paths to follow.

Bess climbed through the grass, in and out of a bush, and through a patch of dandelions. By the time she reached the stream, she could hardly move for all the grass and seeds and fluff sticking to her.

She made her way down the mossy bank to the shore. And then she stopped. How was she going to do this?

Bess knew she should have put aside her pride and let Quill help her wash her wings. It wasn't an easy job for any fairy to do by herself. But at the time, Bess had just wanted Quill to leave.

So now the problem was, what if she fell into the water? She had no idea how deep the water was. But she could see that the stream was running at an impish, happy-to-knock-you-over-and-carry-you- away pace.

Cautiously, she dipped in a toe.

"Ooh!" It was cold!

Still, Bess had little choice. It was much too far to walk back to the Home Tree for a proper bath. So she knelt beside the stream. Cupping her hands, she began to splash water onto herself to try to wash the grass and juice away.

The dried juice in her hair was particularly hard to wash out. Finally, she gave up splashing. She leaned over, ready to stick her whole head in the water.

Crrrooaak!

A frog Bess hadn't noticed leaped into the stream. It landed with a splash. Bess didn't have a chance of keeping her balance. The next thing she knew, she fell headfirst into the water, making quite a splash of her own.

"Sppplugh!"

She kicked and waved and sputtered, even though her bottom was firmly on the stream's pebbled floor. Luckily, the water was not very deep. Yet the harder Bess flailed, the faster the playful stream became. At last it began to carry her away!

"Stop! Let me out!" Bess begged.

By then her wings were impossibly heavy. "Help!" Bess cried. "Help! Help! *Help!*"

"Bess!" a voice called out. "Stop kicking! The stream doesn't like it! Just calm down, and I'll pull you out. What were you *doing?*"

Bess made herself relax. A second later, her friend Rani, a water-talent fairy, pulled her out of the water. Bess was safe, if sopping wet, on a sandy shore.

"Rani, you saved me!" Bess panted, as much with exhaustion as with relief. "You must let me do something for you." She tried to raise herself onto her elbows. But her waterlogged wings felt like weights on her back. She settled for rolling over to face her friend. "I know! How about a – "

" – portrait!" Rani almost shrieked. "Just like Tinker Bell's? Bess, you read our minds! We were just talking about how wonderful it would be for each of us to have a portrait!"

"Each of you?" Bess said, confused.

"Yes, each of us!" Rani replied. "Everyone," she called to a group of water-talent fairies. "Come down here and see Bess. She's going to paint portraits of all of us. We'll be the first talent group to have a complete set!" She teared up with joy. "And could somebody please bring me a leafkerchief?" she asked, sniffing loudly.

In seconds, a dozen eager water fairies surrounded Bess.

"So when can you get started?" Rani asked.

"Well, honestly," Bess began, "I have several others to finish first. And then I'll probably have to make more – "

" – paint!" Rani cut in knowingly. "Of course."

"I hope you'll use *watercolours* for all of our portraits," Silvermist said with a giggle. The whole group of water-talent fairies laughed.

Bess managed to smile politely. She struggled to her feet.

"Oh, here, let me help you," said Rani. "You'll never get anywhere with wings *that* full of water."

She brushed a bit of fairy dust from her arm onto Bess's wings. Then she held her hands above them. Closing her eyes, Rani drew the water out in a thin silvery ribbon. She formed it into a ball and tossed it into the stream.

"Your wings will still be damp for a while," she said, turning back to Bess. "But at least they won't weigh you down."

Bess stood and gave her wings a little flap. "Much better," she said with relief. But her relief turned to dismay as she thought of the new portraits... a whole *talent*'s worth. Goodness!

As she said goodbye to the water fairies,

Bess tried to remind herself that portrait painting was an honour.

"Don't forget about our portraits!" the fairies called after her.

"Oh," said Bess, "I won't."

6

BESS HEADED BACK across the meadow, in the direction of her studio. To her dismay, her flying was a little wobbly since her wings were still a bit damp. *But at least I'm clean,* she thought. She tore off a piece of grass and used it to tie back a lock of hair.

With a sigh, Bess realized that she could use some clean clothes. She hadn't been back to her room in the Home Tree in quite a while. A bit of freshening up in general might do her some good. So she quickly turned away from her studio, towards the Home Tree.

As she neared the knothole door, however, her stomach began to churn. Bess's room was in the tree's south-southwest branch. That meant passing dozens of rooms and workshops. Who knew how many fairies she might meet along the way? And what if they all wanted portraits? Not that Bess didn't want to paint them all. She just wasn't sure she wanted to do it right *now*.

No, going through the Home Tree was *not* the way to get to her room, Bess decided. She would have to sneak in through her back window instead.

Bess had never flown to her room from behind before. But really, how hard could it be? She circled the trunk to the side where the low evening sun was shining. Thank goodness it hadn't set yet! Then she looked up at the rows of brightly coloured window boxes along the tree's branches.

Now, that's a subject for painting, she thought wistfully. But right now, the window boxes were for counting.

"One... two... three... four...

five…"

Bess got to thirteen, but then she had to stop. The Home Tree's leafy branches began to block her view. Bess flew closer and continued counting.

"Fourteen… fifteen… sixteen. Here it is!"

Funny, she thought, *I don't remember that leaf in front of my window.*

Bess flew over to the window and tugged on the sash. Stubbornly, it refused to give. She pulled a little harder. But still the window held fast.

"What am I going to do now?" Bess said. She balled her fists and pounded the window in frustration.

Immediately, the window gave way. Bess tumbled inside.

How odd, she thought, shaking her sore head. *I always thought that window opened out…*

"Bess!" came an alarmed voice from across the room. "Are you all right?"

"Quill!" Bess cried, looking up. "What are you doing here?"

"I'm sculpting – in my room," Quill replied. Her voice now sounded more puzzled than shocked.

"*Your* room?" Bess bit her lip as she rose to her feet. Her eyes darted around the tidy chamber. She looked from one stone sculpture to another, over to the cast-bronze bedstead, and then to the marble busts set into each wall. Finally, her eyes went back to Quill.

"Yes," Quill said. "My room. Did you need something, Bess?"

Bess tried to swallow the lump in her throat. She choked out a laugh. "Need something! Ha! That's a good one, Quill. No. No. No. I was just… er… flying by… to let you know I *don't* need anything! And, uh… "

She looked down at her limp, wrinkled, stained skirt. "To show you that I cleaned up... all by myself!"

She swallowed once more and stretched her mouth into a grin.

"I see," said Quill. She still looked confused. "I'm... so glad."

"Anyway," Bess went on, "I have portraits of all the water-talent fairies to do. I really must fly off."

"Are you sure I can't help you in some way?" Quill asked again.

"Absolutely not," said Bess. Still grinning, she took a backwards hop towards the door... and ran straight into a granite statue of a luna moth. With a crash it fell from its pedestal onto the hard wooden floor.

Bess cringed. "Oh, no!"

"Don't worry." Quill flew over and sprinkled some fairy dust on the heavy statue. Then she used the magic to stand it back up.

"No harm done," she said.

"Truly," said Bess, "I'd fly backwards if I could."

Quill laughed. "Flying backwards is how you knocked it over in the first place."

Bess knew it was a joke. But she couldn't help noticing that Quill hovered protectively next to the moth statue.

Bess blushed. "See you later, Quill," she said. And she hurried out of the room before she could do more damage.

Oh, of all the rooms to fall into by mistake, why did it have to be Quill's? Bess thought as she flew to the next room down the hall. She reached for the knob. Then, just to be safe, she checked the number on the door to make sure it was hers.

Inside, Bess's mood quickly lifted. It was a relief to be among her favourite things.

She flew to her bed, which was covered

in a multi coloured quilt made from different kinds of flower petals. She lay back and gazed up at the stained-glass window above her. The sun was almost down, but there was just enough light to allow the colours to dance along the wall across the room.

And, oh, the walls! They were covered with framed pictures of every shape and size. Many were gifts from other art fairies. The rest were drawings and paintings that Bess had done herself. There was her very first sketch of Mother Dove. Next to it hung her Home Tree series. She'd followed the tree through all its seasons – spring and summer (which were the only seasons in Never Land).

Each work reminded Bess of a time and place and mood. Some were good and some were bad, but each was special in its own way.

Then her eyes fell on a statue in the corner. It was a portrait of Bess carved out of smooth sandalwood. Quill had given it to her as a gift on her last Arrival Day anniversary. Quill had remembered how much more Bess liked wood than hard, cold stone.

Bess smiled at the statue. It was a perfect likeness, right down to Bess's long fringe and the paintbrush behind her ear.

Funny, Bess thought. She yawned and let her heavy eyelids close for just a moment. *If I didn't know better, I'd say that was the work of a good friend.*

7

THE NEXT THING SHE KNEW, Bess awoke to a loud knock at her door. She didn't even remember falling asleep! What time was it?

Knock-knock-knock.

"Bess! Are you in there?"

Groggily, Bess flew up and opened the door.

"Hi, Bess! It's me! Is it done?"

It was Dulcie.

"I went to your studio. Your sign said you'd be there this morning. But when you never showed up, I thought maybe I'd find you here."

"Oh," said Bess. She pushed her hair out of her eyes, trying to wake up.

"*So?*" Dulcie went on. "Is it done?"

"Is what done?"

"My portrait!"

"Oh!" Bess thought for a moment. "As a

matter of fact, it is. But it's not here, of course. It's back at my studio."

"Well, come on!" Dulcie grabbed her arm. "Let's go!"

By the time they reached the tangerine crate, Bess was wide awake. She was pleased to be presenting the new portrait.

She had to admit, though, that she was a little disappointed that Dulcie hadn't brought another plate of rolls, or some other tasty treat.

"I came as soon as I woke up!" Dulcie explained excitedly, almost as if she could read Bess's thoughts. "I haven't even been to the kitchen yet to bake."

"Really?" Bess was touched. How important this was to Dulcie! "Let's take a look, then, shall we?" she said.

She led Dulcie to a row of easels, each draped with a thick velvet-moss cloth. With a quick flick of the wrist, and just the right touch of drama and modesty (something every art fairy arrives with), she yanked off the cover of the nearest one.

"Ooh!" Dulcie fluttered up and down. She clapped her hands. "I love it! I love it!" she gushed. "I can practically taste those poppy puff rolls right now!" And as if to test them, she reached out to touch the painting. Then she stopped.

"What? What is it?" asked Bess.

"Do my wings really stick up like that at the back?" Dulcie asked. The joy slowly drained from her face.

"What do you mean?" said Bess.

"My wings!" said Dulcie. "They're... *huge*." She strained her neck, trying to see behind herself. "They're not really that big, are they?"

"Actually, they are," came a cheerful voice from just outside the door. "Good morning, Bess. Dulcie. Is my portrait ready, too?"

"Hello, Rosetta," replied Bess. She was still stunned by Dulcie's reaction. "Er, yes. Yours is done, too."

While Dulcie anxiously compared her wings with those in the painting, Bess reached for the second velvet cover and pulled it off.

Rosetta beamed. Then a tiny wrinkle formed between her brows.

"How do you like the lilies of the valley?" Bess asked. "I tried to make each one practically perfect, just like yours, but not so perfect that they wouldn't look real."

"Oh, yes, they're very nice," Rosetta said. Still, she looked concerned. "It's just ... my *nose*. I know for a fact that it's much prettier than *that*."

Dulcie glanced away from her portrait. "Actually, it's not."

Rosetta frowned. "Yes, it is. Would you mind, Bess," she went on, "going back and straightening my nose... and maybe taking a little off the sides?"

"Oh, yes!" said Dulcie. "Could you make my wings smaller, too, Bess? That would be wonderful!"

Bess's mouth fell open. Every fairy had her opinions. But Bess had never before been asked to change her art. Like all talents, she prided herself on doing her best from the very beginning. What were these fairies thinking?

But Bess didn't even have time to reply before a dozen more fairies swooped into her studio, each one eager to see her brand-new portrait. And each one, Bess could tell, was eager to offer her honest opinion.

By the time the fairies had left, Bess was drained – and hungry.

She looked at the sun outside her

window. It was high in the sky. She had probably missed breakfast by a good hour. But perhaps a few kind serving-talents would still be serving tea.

Bess hoped so.

As soon as she reached the Home Tree, she flew straight through the main hall and down the long corridor to the tearoom.

She headed directly for the art-talent fairies' table. As she had feared, the other art-talent fairies had finished their breakfast and returned to their own studios. Most of the tables in the tearoom were empty, in fact. The cleaning-talent fairies were busy taking dirty teacups and breakfast trays away.

"Bessy, dear!" called Laidel, a serving-talent fairy. She swooped up beside Bess. "We were afraid you weren't coming. Let me bring you some tea. And maybe a scone?"

"That would be lovely," said Bess, sinking into a chair.

"Coming right up!" said Laidel.

In moments, the fairy was back. Her tray was piled high with Bess's favourite tea, sweet cream and clover honey, heart-shaped currant – *Ugh!* Bess thought – scones, blueberry muffins with freshly churned butter, and a tall stack of buckwheat pancakes dripping with warm syrup.

"I thought you looked a bit tired, Bess," said Laidel. "So I brought you a little extra." She gave Bess a wink as she poured a stream of tea into a cup. She set it down before Bess. "Don't tell the other fairies!"

Bess smiled at her gratefully and took a sip. "Ahh! Just what I needed."

"I'm so glad," said Laidel. "Now, just sit back, relax, and enjoy your tea. There you go. I'll come back in a little while and we can talk about my portrait."

Pwahhh! Bess's eyes popped open and the tea she'd been sipping sprayed across the tablecloth. Her cup fell to the floor, where the rest of the tea made a stain on the floral carpet.

Bess reached down to mop it up with her napkin. But another hand, clutching a springy moss sponge, beat her to it.

"Allow me," said Colin, a rather tall (in fairy terms) and rather plump (in any terms) cleaning-talent sparrow man. He dabbed at the spill until no trace of tea was left. Then he flew off with the empty cup and returned in an instant with a new one.

"If there's anything else I can do for you, Bess," he said with a bow, "let me know."

"I will," said Bess.

"For instance," Colin went on, "if you'd

like me to pose for one of your portraits, just ask. I'm sure you don't come across a model like *me* every day!"

Bess shook her head. "Er, no, I don't," she said. "But to tell you the truth, Colin, I don't need any more models today. I'm a little behind, I'm afraid."

"No problem," Colin said with a shrug. "We'll do it tomorrow." With a smile, he turned. "Hey, Elda!" he called to a cleaning-talent fairy across the room. "I talked to Bess. She says we should come by her studio *tomorrow!*"

Bess poured a new cup of tea. But the joy of the meal had gone away. Not even the buckwheat pancakes (which had always been Bess's favourite) tasted good.

Maybe I should leave, she thought. *I should get busy painting again. Besides, who knows how many more portraits I'll have to do if I stay!*

But it was too late. Suddenly, a whole line of eager fairies flew out of the kitchen – baking talents, dish-washing talents, silver-polishing talents, serving talents, and everyone else who happened to be around.

"Hi, Bess," called Dulcie. "Colin said you were here. Did you like the scones? I told everyone in the kitchen about my portrait. And don't you know, now they all want one!"

"Oh, yes!" said another baking-talent fairy. "We've each got to have a portrait, too!"

Bess tried not to groan. But it hardly would have mattered if she had. The fairies were busy chattering with each other, describing *exactly* how they wanted their portraits to be.

"Just be sure to keep your wings tucked in," Dulcie said knowingly.

Finally, Bess held up her hands.

"Friends," she began, "I am truly, truly

honoured by your regard for my work. But I'm not sure I can paint all your portraits right now. Maybe a quick sketch would do?" she asked hopefully.

The fairies looked at one another.

"No," said one silver-polisher. "We want *portraits*, like everyone else."

"Yes!" the others chimed in. "We want portraits! We want portraits! We want portraits!"

8

BESS LEFT THE TEAROOM with sixteen more portraits to do.

She hoped she'd have enough paint. But as she pulled one, and then another, paintbrush from the pouch at her waist, she realized she would definitely need more brushes.

Vole hair made the best paintbrushes. Bess could usually find patches of it near the edge of the forest. (Those voles just moult like crazy.) The forest was not far from her studio. She decided that she should fly by and collect some on her way.

And she was so glad she did. The light was *gorgeous*! It was streaming through the trees, casting deep, dark shadows that were so… interesting!

Back to business, Bess reminded herself over and over.

But where were all the vole hairs?

Then, at last, just when Bess thought she would have to make do with dandelion fluff, she spotted a tuft of tiny gray hairs stuck to a blade of grass.

She darted over and began to collect them. All of a sudden, she felt a firm, sharp peck on the top of her head!

"Chrrrp-chrrrp! Trillillillillill!"

Bess spun around to see a stern grey bird staring at her. It was twice as big as she was.

"Eeeek!" shrieked Bess.

"Eeeek!" chirped the bird. *"Chrrr-chrrr-chrrrp-trrrillll!"*

A voice rose from the shadows. "She says she needs those hairs for her nest."

Bess looked to the right and saw a reddish brown head poke out from behind a short stump.

"Fawn," Bess said. "I'd fly backward if I

could. I didn't know."

"That's okay," Fawn replied. She was an animal-talent fairy. She could talk to animals in their own languages. "These mockingbirds are a little testy. But they don't mean any harm. Just looking out for their babies."

Bess rubbed the sore spot on her head. "I see." She watched the bird pluck the hairs with her beak.

"Do you think she could spare a few hairs for a new paintbrush?" Bess asked Fawn.

Fawn grinned and turned to the bird. Together, they twittered and chirped for a good three or four minutes. Then the fairy turned back to Bess and nodded.

"Take as many as you need," Fawn said.

"That's kind of her!" said Bess. "What in Never Land did you say?"

Fawn grinned again. "I just told her what a fantastic and famous fairy artist you are.

And that you needed hairs for a new paintbrush. *And* that if she shared hers, you would paint her portrait!" She winked at Bess and whispered, "She's quite vain, you know. Oh, and I also told her you would paint me, too."

"Paint you?" said Bess.

"Would you?" asked Fawn. "Everyone is talking about your portraits, and I've never had one done. I just saw Madge's. I don't care how much she thinks she looks like a dragonfly – I think it's wonderful! What a great talent you have! Tell me" – Fawn paused and wrapped her arms fondly around the bird – "do you want to paint us here? Or back at your studio?"

"Right now?" Bess said.

"Why not?" said Fawn with a shrug. "It's early. Besides," she went on with a nod towards the mockingbird, "it's the only way you're going to get your vole hairs."

With a halfhearted sigh, Bess sank onto a patch of moss. She pulled some pencils and her sketchbook from her smock. "I'll *sketch* you here," she told the eager pair. "Then I'll paint you back at my studio. *Alone.*"

The mockingbird warbled something to Fawn. "Be sure to paint her right side – it's her best," Fawn translated. "See, what did I tell you? Oh! And when you do me, don't feel as if you have to make my teeth so big, you know? There are some fairies who call me Chipmunk. Can you believe it?"

Bess began her sketch, just as she'd done for all the fairies.

But she soon found her interest drifting away from her models and off to the forest.

The sun slowly shifted across the late-morning sky. A gentle breeze swept up and blew a flock of woolly clouds across the blue horizon. Closer to the forest's edge, shadows shivered and danced about on the ground.

And then, the west wind kicked in. At first, it was refreshing. But Never winds are fickle and prone to mischief, especially those from the west. And this one was no different.

It began by blowing all the dandelions' fluff off their stalks, leaving their bald-headed stems to flap about. Then it moved into the trees. It worked the leaves into a rustling frenzy. It sent acorns and hickory nuts crashing to the ground.

Feathers flying, the mockingbird did her best to hold her ground – and her good side. Fawn clung to her neck with all her might.

"Uh, Bess! Shall we call it a day?" Fawn hollered over the din.

"Hold on!" Bess called back. She was sketching furiously in her book. "I'm almost done."

"I *can't* hold on!" Fawn cried.

The mockingbird let out a stream

of frantic chirps. The wind gleefully carried away half of them. But Fawn understood.

"She has to get back to her nest, Bess," Fawn shouted. "Crazy wind! Her babies are scared!"

Bess sighed. Fawn was right. They all should go. Besides, by now it wasn't easy to keep her sketchbook from blowing away.

She said goodbye to the mockingbird, who swiftly flew off to her chicks. Fawn asked a chipmunk to carry her and Bess home. And off they rode. Bess held her book of sketches tightly. Her heart was full of newfound joy.

Then the wind died away.

9

BESS COULDN'T WAIT to start painting!

She was bursting with inspiration. Her brushes flew about the canvas.

It wasn't until she stepped back from it that Bess realized that what she had painted wasn't a portrait at all. It was the forest, as she had seen it, in all its pinwheels of texture and colour. Great swirls of greens and blues, whites and browns, bright yellows and mysterious greys filled her canvas.

Oh, but it was satisfying! So full of energy and life. Bess hadn't felt this good since she'd finished Tink's portrait. *What's the difference?* she wondered. *What has been missing from all my paintings lately?*

Bess left her studio and flew towards the Home Tree. On her way, she saw a message-talent fairy. Bess stopped her.

"Do you think you could ask everyone

to gather in the courtyard today, just before teatime?" Bess asked her. "The light should be perfect for the unveiling of my newest painting! It's a masterpiece!"

"Of course," the message-talent fairy said, and she quickly flew off.

Bess counted the minutes until teatime. She couldn't help staring at the masterpiece. Any fairy who appreciated fine painting would absolutely *love* it! She was sure.

Bess's new painting was quite large by fairy standards – five by seven inches. She sprinkled it with fairy dust to make it easier to carry. Then she covered it with a piece of silky cloth and set off for the courtyard of the Home Tree.

Bess had planned on being the first fairy to arrive. But to her surprise, the courtyard was practically full. Everyone was eager to see Bess's great masterpiece.

"It might be a portrait of me!" a dust-talent fairy told a water-talent fairy.

"Or it might be of Fawn," said an animal-talent fairy. "I heard that Bess wouldn't stop sketching her this morning – despite a windstorm!"

"I don't know," someone else said. "It's so large. Perhaps it's *all* of us!"

Finally, it was time. Bess flew up to call everyone to order. Her glow was practically white with excitement.

She smiled at the crowd. "I think you will be glad you flew here today... especially considering what art lovers you all have become! It is because you appreciate art that I couldn't wait to share my newest painting with you. And so... " Bess grabbed the cloth. She yanked it away with a flourish. "I call it... *Swept Away!*"

In the courtyard, there was silence.

Bess looked happily at her painting.

Then she turned to her fans. But the faces staring back at her were blank.

"That's not *me*," she heard one or two fairies mumble.

"That's not me, either," echoed several more.

"No, of course!" Bess chuckled. "It's not any of you. It's... it's a feeling I had of being swept away! In the forest... in the moment... in my art! Isn't it wonderful?"

"It's *what?*" she heard Fawn call out.

"It's a feeling," Bess repeated.

Honestly! Bess's forehead wrinkled in frustration. She began to explain once more – but before she could say another word, the tea chimes rang.

"Teatime!" called Laidel.

"We're coming," several fairies cried in reply.

"Very nice, Bess," said a few water-talent fairies politely as they flew by. Bess looked for tears of emotion. But their eyes were surprisingly dry.

The other art-talent fairies applauded her. But even they seemed more eager than usual to make their way inside.

"Wait!" Bess meekly called. Where were all the adoring fairies? Where were all the requests for paintings of their own? Fiddlesticks! Where were all the compliments Bess had... well... got used to?

Within minutes, the courtyard was empty. Bess's glow faded from white to a dull, disappointed mustard colour.

She felt her chin begin to tremble. Her eyes welled up with tears.

"Darling, I sincerely hope you're not *crying*. Don't we get enough of that with those pitiful water-talent fairies?"

Bess sniffled and looked up. She saw Vidia flying over.

"I'm not in the mood for your

comments right now, Vidia," she managed to say, despite the lump in her throat.

"Suit yourself," said the fairy, turning to go. "I really didn't want to tell you anyway that I liked your painting."

"You *what?*" Bess said with a gasp.

"I like it," replied Vidia, looking back over her shoulder. "And I'd appreciate it, sweetheart, if you didn't make me say it again."

"Wait!" Bess called out. "Don't go! Stay!" She watched in amazement as the fairy zipped back towards her. "So you really like it?"

Vidia rolled her eyes. "Yes," she said.

Bess grinned. "*Ah.* At least someone does."

"Why, Bess, dear, don't you like it?"

"Well... " Bess stopped to consider Vidia's question. "Yes, I do. I like it very much."

"So there you are. Of course, I can see why you would value *my* opinion. But do you really care so much what those silly slowpokes think?" Vidia scoffed. "Really. And here I thought you were an artist."

It was hard to agree with someone as unpleasant as Vidia. *But she has a point,* Bess thought. Bess loved her painting, and she'd loved painting it. And wasn't that really what art was all about? How could she have let herself forget so easily?

"Um, Vidia," she said. Her hands nervously twisted the cloth that had covered her painting. "Would you, by any chance, like to have this painting?"

For a split second, Vidia actually looked pleased. But her pale face quickly hardened into a scowl. "Darling, are you giving me a present?" she said haughtily. "What in Never Land have I ever done for *you?*"

"You told me the truth," Bess replied. "But more than that, my painting reached you. So I want you to have it."

Vidia's cold eyes moved from Bess to the enormous canvas. And Bess could see them faintly warming.

"I'll take good care of it," Vidia said finally. Then she took a pinch of fairy dust from the pouch hanging from her belt and sprinkled it onto the painting. Picking the painting up, she darted away.

Smiling, Bess watched her go. Then she took a deep breath and braced herself for the difficult task ahead.

10

BESS COULD SMELL the freshly baked honey buns and butter cookies even before she got to the tearoom. But that day, tea would have to wait until after her announcement.

She hated to think about how the other fairies would react. The best thing to do, she told herself, was not think too hard – just do it.

She flew to the front of the great room. She stood between the wide floor-to-ceiling windows and flapped her wings for attention.

"Everyone!" she called. "Everyone! I have an announcement."

The clink of china and the hum of voices, however, did not grow any fainter.

"I *said*," Bess shouted, "I have an important announcement to make!"

One of her wings accidentally knocked over a tea tray. At last, someone took notice.

"Oh, fairies!" Laidel called out. She clinked a spoon against a cup. "I think Bess has something to say."

The noise died down. All eyes turned to Bess.

"Uh… " Bess was suddenly nervous. How was she going to do this? She wished that she had written her announcement down.

"I… I just wanted to tell you all that I realized something important this morning – something I somehow let myself forget." She brushed her fringe out of her eyes. "The joy of my talent comes not *just* from painting, you see. It comes from painting what *inspires* me, *when* it inspires me. I think that is something you all can understand. I must be true to my talent, and to myself. And so" – Bess drew a deep breath – "although it has been a great honour to be asked to paint so many of your portraits, I won't be able to finish them for quite a while."

Bess closed her eyes. She waited for the backlash.

Clink, clank, slurrrp.

Bess slowly opened one eye, and then the other. All around the room, the fairies had gone back to their tea.

"Wait!" Bess blurted out. "Did you all hear what I said?"

"Oh, yes," several fairies replied.

"We sure did," said a few more.

"You need to be inspired," Laidel said. "We completely understand."

"I know!" said Dulcie, flying by with a plate of fresh rolls. "Maybe you'd be inspired by Hem's new dress! Stand up, Hem, and show her!"

A plump-cheeked, white-haired fairy modestly stood up. She modelled her dress made of soft pink peony petals. It was tight in the waist and full down to the knees. Hem wore open-toed pink slippers dyed to match. Although Bess liked clothes that were more flowy and colourful, she had to agree that it was very nice.

"Oh, isn't it gorgeous!" cooed Rosetta from the table next to her.

"I've got to have one!" said another garden-talent fairy.

"Me too!" more fairies chimed in.

"Me first, though!" said Dulcie. "Hem promised to make one for me first. Didn't you, Hem? First fairy to come, first fairy served!"

Soon a ring four fairies deep had formed around poor Hem. Teatime – and Bess – had been forgotten.

Bess sank into a nearby chair. She stared, bewildered, at the scene. Could it be that Bess and her portraits had lost all their importance? Had she awakened any real art appreciation in the fairies? Or had her art been just a… just a *fad*?

The idea made her wings limp. Bess's spirits sank. Oh, the horror!

She buried her head in her arms, in case a tear should fall.

"Bess?"

She felt a cool hand on her shoulder.

"Why don't you come to our table?"

Slowly, Bess looked up into Quill's eyes. Her spirits sank even lower. As if making a complete fool of herself wasn't bad enough. Did she have to do it right in front of Quill *again*?

"I saved you two star-shaped butter cookies. But if you don't eat them quickly, Linden will."

Bess sniffled a little and shook her head. "I'm not hungry," she said. "I don't know if I'll ever be hungry again."

"Oh, yes, you will," Quill said.

Bess pushed back her fringe. She sniffled once more. "How can you be so sure?"

"Because – " Quill began.

But before she could finish, she was interrupted by Hem's high-pitched voice from the far end of the room. "One at a time, fairies! Please! One at a time!"

Bess and Quill looked over at the ever-widening circle around the dressmaking fairy. They couldn't help smiling at each other.

Quill leaned towards Bess. "Remind me to tell you about the time, a few years before you arrived, when all the fairies decided they just *had* to have their very own tiny hand-carved talent symbols to wear around their necks."

"Really?" Bess was surprised. "That sounds lovely! But... I don't think I've ever seen one."

Quill grinned and nodded. "Exactly."

"*Ah!*" It took a moment, but Bess got it. "Fairies!"

Maybe I will have a cookie or two after all, Bess thought. And maybe she *would* paint Hem's cute pink dress. Perhaps with a bright green background! Or should it be orange? Or maybe she'd paint something else that day. Or do something with clay? She could even carve with Quill.

There was one thing for sure, though. From then on, whatever Bess did, it would be her choice – and hers alone.